SULLY'S
FANTASY

Sully's Fantasy

Goddess Isles
Novella

by

Pepper Winters

Published: Pepper Winters 2020: **pepperwinters@gmail.com**
Cover Design: Ari @ Cover it! Designs
Editing by: Editing 4 Indies (Jenny Sims)

Dedicated to:

*Those who use books for a portal to another existence, era, and experience.
Words are magic, and I'm so grateful you're reading mine.*

Sullivan

Prologue

EVERYONE HAD A PAST.

Some were secrets we liked to hide, others were triumphs we liked to brag about, and others…others were just journeys—steps we took to find who we were, what we stood for, and what sort of mark we wanted to leave behind. Along the way, there were mistakes and challenges, and sometimes, even catastrophic things like death and betrayal.

A lot of people have said that 'life is about the journey and not the destination', and I agreed with that…to a degree.

My life was still on a journey—it would be until I took my last breath—but now, instead of walking my path alone, I'd found the one person who made everything infinitely more bearable.

It wasn't a monetary achievement or career accolade or any other accomplishment that triggered the end of my journey.

It was her.

A girl I bought and kidnapped.

A goddess who I commanded and manipulated.

A woman who cured me of my sins.

Eleanor Grace, Eleanor *Sinclair*, was my destination.

With her by my side and her hand in my mine, I didn't fucking care where the journey took us. We could walk into squalor and famine, and I would smile because she was beside me.

Through thick and thin, Eleanor had my back, my trust, and my entire fucking heart.

And I had her.

Every part of her.

And I didn't like sharing.

Good thing we were island recluses these days, and when we did have to travel, Euphoria gave us somewhere to be just us.

A dimension where no one else existed.

A fantasy where anything was possible.

Chapter One

TIME WAS RELATIVE.

Make something enjoyable, and time was forgotten. Those tight clusters of minutes vanished because we were present in that singular moment. Entirely consumed by the experience we found enjoyable. However, change enjoyable to painful, and time became far too noticeable. Those tight clusters quadrupled, so a moment lasted four times as long. Human nature caused us to fight against the clock, to be free of that painful situation and run.

I'd experienced both in my life.

When I was younger, there'd been the shortness of school holidays, and the eternity of stressful exams.

And then, of course, there'd been the kidnapping.

The men who'd grabbed me in the kitchen of the backpackers, where my boyfriend and I were staying, had caused time to slow to a terrifying crawl. It abandoned me to the dark cell I was held in and didn't start ticking again until I was flown to Goddess Isles and met the man who'd purchased me.

But the moment our eyes met?

Time ignited and disintegrated. Every clock smashed. Every minute hand broke into pieces. Why? Because time was no longer needed.

Time was the structure that all humanity and nature marched to, but love…love had the power of cutting you free. It erased all notion of time because it honestly didn't exist for us anymore.

We'd found each other.

Our countdown was over, and we lived side by side in bliss.

"Jinx…what are you mooning over now?"

Sully's rough baritone ripped me from my musings, making me blink and squint in the bright Indonesian sun. Raising an arm, well-tanned from living in the tropics and ignoring the constant glitter of sand upon my skin from living on an island, I grinned at my sexy husband. "Not mooning, thinking."

"Uh-huh." Sully rolled his stunning blue eyes and scratched at this thick five o'clock shadow. "Well, whatever you were thinking about, snap out of it. I asked you a question, so give me an answer, woman."

I padded toward him, barefoot with just a wraparound cream dress encasing a silver bikini beneath. This impromptu visit to *Serigala* had turned from a fleeting inspection into an all-day excursion.

"What was the question?" I stopped beside him, trailing my hand in the manmade pool that housed shallows, caverns, and aquatic dens perfect for the tenants currently healing within.

With my fingers dangling in the warm water, I smiled as a shy shadow moved toward the surface. Sully wrapped his arm around me as the mimic octopus drifted closer, it's graceful swim and small body melting my heart like it did every time I'd visited.

"And you say I'm the one with power over animals," Sully murmured as a small octopus reached out with a tentative tentacle and wrapped it around my pinkie. The sensation of its tiny suckers and the silkiness of its sinuous arms never failed to cause wonder.

"He's just come to trust me, that's all."

"Wrong. It's because he can sense you're *trustworthy*."

"You're the one who saved him. Saved all of them."

"*We* saved them." He pressed a kiss to my temple as a second octopus floated from its hidey-hole and descended into my palm, wrapping its tiny tentacles around my wrist, and curling out of the water like strange flower fronds.

Both mimics were speckled light brown, muted and content. However, when they hunted or were chased, they could mimic so many things—not just in colour camouflage but movement too.

They could swim like a flatfish, or stalk like a lionfish, or even threaten like a venomous sea snake. I'd done research on the critters ever since Sully had been called to rescue five of them when sea dredging on the main island dumped them from their home, leaving one dead, two seriously injured, and two traumatised.

I'd visited often in that first week of healing and found them utterly fascinating. The fact that they'd only been noticed in the late 90s was a testament to how well they could mimic their underwater world and stay hidden, and the level of intelligence in their quizzical gaze made me think they'd willingly hold a conversation with me if we spoke the same tongue.

The first mimic uncoiled its tentacle from my pinkie in favour of squeezing my thumb. A flash of brown and white over his body warned the other octopus that he'd claimed me.

The other octopus, missing a tentacle and still wounded from the dredgers, puffed up to twice its size and crawled up my arm out of the water.

Sully chuckled. "Guess I have some competition for your affection."

I grinned and offered my other hand, transferring the suckered tentacles to my free palm and then placing him back underwater. "They've certainly made me fall for slippery things." I laughed as the two octopuses squeezed my fingers, then slipped away, sinking to the bottom where they ruffled up the sand in search of snacks.

"They'll be released in a month. They're almost ready." Sully waited as I rinsed off my hands and wiped them on my dress. He didn't reprimand about the price tag of my clothing or make me feel as if I should take more care. He just grinned and clamped both hands on my hips to scoot me to face him.

His head ducked, his nose nuzzled mine, and his lips pressed sweetly to my mouth.

I kissed him back.

Soft to start and then harder as he slipped his tongue inside me and quested a deeper kind of connection.

My heart instantly raced. My core liquefied. My entire body set off fireworks. Our conduit of connection hummed with quick-fire need. I moaned, reaching up to run my fingers through his hair.

He pulled away, running his tongue along his bottom lip. "Christ, you turn me on."

"You can't keep doing that," I whispered.

"Keep doing what?" He arched his hips into mine, showing it wasn't just me affected by our spontaneous kiss.

"Keep making me lose my mind every time you kiss me.

You'd think I'd be bored of kissing you after all this time."

"Bored?" He scowled with mock offensive. "After five years of marriage, you're saying you want to replace me?"

I laughed. "I'm saying, after five years of marriage, I keep expecting this chemistry to fade a little…after all, I do know everything about you now. I know your deepest, darkest secrets."

"My only secret these days is that I want you all the goddamn time." He pressed his hips harder into mine. "And that chemistry you're complaining about is one of the things I love most about us."

"The fact that we can't keep our hands off each other?" I grinned. "That we have a reputation of improper obsession? That the staff whisper behind our backs that we're high on whatever drugs you've been cooking, and it's made us incapable of surviving without being in each other's pocket?"

"Precisely." He chuckled, letting me go and taking my hand to lead me back through the rebuilt sanctuary of *Serigala*. After Drake's bomb five years ago, we'd taken our time to landscape, design, and hire the right people. The island was once again a fully equipped, highly successful rehab facility for broken and abused animals. "In fact, I need access to your pockets right now."

"I'm wearing a dress. It doesn't have pockets."

"It's a metaphor, Jinx. I need inside *your* pocket. Your hot, wet—"

"Behave." I swatted his arm. "You had me last night."

He threw me a rakish smirk. "Exactly. That was *hours* ago. I need you. Otherwise, the whispers that I can't survive without you will prove true, and I'll die right here."

"I swear you weren't always this dramatic or mischievous."

Guiding me forward, he threw me a besotted, heart-stopping look. "You improved me."

"I broke you more like."

"You married me."

"Same thing."

He let out a massive laugh, making my insides flutter and my body tingle.

I laughed too. "By the way, what was your question that was ever so important five minutes ago?"

"Don't know. Don't care. I want you."

"Anything to do with *Serigala*? An animal? A vet?"

Sully frowned before recalling. "There's a Chinese cosmetic company that's finally shutting down its animal testing—after our campaign and immense social media pressure. They have hundreds of rabbits, rats, and a few chinchillas that need rehabbing."

"And you wanted to know if we have space for that many new arrivals?"

"I wanted to make sure you were okay taking on several more hundred lives."

I stroked his cheek. "You should by now that you don't need to ask, Sully. After all, you have a few more vacant islands. We have room to spread. *Of course*, I'm fine with them coming here. The more the merrier."

"And now I want you all the more, woman." He ducked and kissed me, his tongue aggressive with want and affection.

I pushed him away, my heart dancing. "If you're that determined, let's go home and find somewhere private."

"Finally, you agree." He smirked, capturing my hand and kissing my knuckles. "Let's go."

We smiled and strode toward the hustle and bustle of Indonesian helpers, vet assistants, and habitats.

So far, *Serigala* was an island where any animal—fanged, farmed, or forgotten—could come to receive vet care, heal, and be placed in a safe forever after home or released back into its natural environment. We'd expanded from the vet care I'd opened on *Batari* while Sully was in a coma and were almost at full capacity on *Serigala*. Last year, excavation work had begun on yet another one of Sully's islands. *Kapu-Kapu*, Indo for butterfly, would officially start housing all manner of creatures in a few months.

It didn't matter how many animals needed our help, we would offer them all sanctuary.

Local staff nodded and smiled as Sully and I made our way through the compound with its spacious pens and shelters where even a Sumatran Tiger was housed away from the herbivores like orangutans that'd been a part of a black market pet ring. The tiger had been seized by law enforcement when a large drug cartel was dismantled in Bali. It'd been so badly mistreated that two paws had to be amputated and an eye removed.

Luckily, he was healing and learning to trust he was safe now. I was grateful we'd been able to take away his pain and give him peace, and hopefully, we'd be able to grant him a wild existence, even with his disabilities.

If not, he would always be safe with us, reminding me all over again how disgusting some humans were. I'd lost my temper a few times on assholes who believed their life was worth more than others. I'd morphed into Sully and effectively hated the human race for their selfishness and entitlement.

Every day, I listed the things I was grateful for, and living in the middle of the Java Sea away from society—where even Google Earth didn't have our coordinates—was high on the list.

Sully being at the top of that very long list, of course.

A couple of years ago, I'd travelled with Sully to America to attend a few days of board meetings that he couldn't do via online conferences. I'd stood by his side as he'd addressed his head scientists, guided new trials, and approved that year's business plan. Just those few days, tucked in a skyscraper and breathing in city carcinogens, were enough to make me claustrophobic.

His pharmaceutical company, Sinclair and Sinclair Group, had been impressive. The tour of floors after floors of high-tech labs had shown me another side to the man I'd fallen in love with and married.

But it also made me appreciate how similar Sully and I had become.

We appreciated where we came from. We understood that we were human and had to play the role we'd been given. However, we were so far from large corporation-controlled masses now that we would never fit in. We were no longer fit for acceptable society.

And that was fine by us.

On the third day in America, we'd attempted to go for a romantic dinner and then a movie. To do what so many other couples did. However, we'd lasted as long as the appetisers before we wordlessly agreed to run.

To run back to the airport and leave a day early. To run away from crippling civilisation that we no longer understood. The second we took off, we'd attacked each other. Ravenous to reconnect, using every inch of his private plane to join the mile-high club, drugged on lust and drunk on the knowledge we were going back to our paradise *alone*.

Waving at Kaly—a local vet nurse who'd done wonders with the latest shipment of chimpanzees and beagles we'd received—I padded beside Sully to the other side of the island where the helicopter waited to take us home.

Not for the first time, and probably not for the last, my stomach twisted a little as Sully hoisted me into the plush interior and kissed my wrist before climbing in himself. The image of him framed in the doorway brought back heart-hiccupping memories.

Of him falling toward the sea.

Of him splashing into the ocean and left for dead.

Of Drake taking me to Geneva to—

"Hey, stop it." His hand landed on my knee, squeezing. "I'm not a fan of helicopters myself these days, but nothing is going to happen to either of us."

I smiled and nodded, wriggling my way into the harness as the pilots turned on the engine and activated the ear-splintering whirring. "I know."

Buckling himself in, Sully once again took my hand as we swooped into the sky. We looked down upon the rows of enclosures and lives we'd saved. No longer able to see the flame scorched earth or the bomb ravaged buildings but celebrating that good had triumphed over evil, and Sully was right.

Drake was dead.

That part of our lives was over.

We were safe. Our animals were safe.

Life was perfect.

Sullivan

Chapter Two

"COME WALK WITH ME?"

Two days after our visit to *Serigala*, I looked up from the text-heavy PDF about a promising drug to treat Alzheimer's. The reading glasses I used these days slid down my nose as I looked up at the most stunning creature I'd ever seen.

Thanks to Drake putting God knew what into my eyes when he'd tortured me, I struggled in certain lights. Most of the time, I could see fine, but at night or if I'd been on my computer for too long, a haze appeared. Then again, I could just be getting old.

After all, I just celebrated my thirty-eighth birthday.

I wasn't old, old by any means, but I wasn't a spring chicken either. Not nearly as young as my delectable wife. I had eleven years on her. Eleven years where I'd existed and she hadn't. Thank hell she was born, even a few years late, because I would've lived a lonely fucking life if she hadn't.

Eleanor stood with her hands on her hips in an open bronze kimono that showed honey golden skin, willowy legs, and toned stomach. Her breasts filled out her black bikini and her hair—the same hair that I found such a fucking turn-on—spilled over one shoulder in a twisted chocolate rope.

Five years we'd been married, and in that time, she hadn't cut it. She'd requested I trim it occasionally to keep the ends tidy, but every day on my shores, she seemed more and more wild. Stunning in her simplicity, breath-stealing in her natural beauty.

Tossing my e-tablet onto the deck lounger where I sat overlooking Nirvana as the waterfall splashed and crashed in the moonlight, I swallowed a sudden growl. "You come to me looking like that and think a *walk* is what I want?"

She grinned, running her hand through her gorgeous hair. "I deliberately wore this to bribe you into a walk. If that walk ends with me pinned against a palm tree, then so be it." Her grey eyes sparkled as Pika and Skittles darted from the lounge behind her.

She laughed as Pika dive-bombed my hair and Skittles chirped loudly in my ear. The two cheeky caiques were on her side it seemed.

Adjusting my rapidly hardening cock, I swung my legs to the deck and stood. My legs had healed from the multiple broken bones, also courtesy of Drake, and to anyone other than my wife, I walked strong and sure.

Eleanor was the only one who noticed my slight limp, thanks to the scar tissue left behind from the harpoon wound. I didn't need the cane she'd had made for me these days, but it still rested by my bed as a memory of the weeks of care she'd given me, all while I'd struggled to stay alive and return to her.

Her eyes raked over me, her tongue licking her lips. "You are a stunning specimen of a man."

I let her feast on me. "I aim to please."

"Oh, you do, you definitely do." Her hungry gaze found the growing bulge between my legs.

Like Eleanor, I was mostly undressed. That was the beauty of living in the tropics. Just black board-shorts required. Convenient when I wanted her. So fucking easy to shed a single layer and pounce, instead of navigating through jackets and jeans and underwear of more civilised city folk. "I think I'll skip the walk." Removing my glasses, I let them fall to the empty deck lounger behind me. "Come here."

"Nope." She held out her hand. "Let's walk to my old villa and swim in the sea."

"We have a perfectly good waterfall here. Let's swim in that." I stepped toward her. "Let's fuck in that."

Her grey eyes sparkled with lusty smoke. "I feel like saltwater instead of fresh." Licking her lips, she added, "You could fuck me on the beach."

My stomach clenched as my cock hardened further. "It seems

you're still a master at putting curses on me." I fisted my thickening erection. "This is your doing, and I can't walk while I'm so hard. Put me out of my misery and—"

"Patience makes everything sweeter." Grabbing my wrist, she tugged my hand away from my cock and yanked me through our villa. The driftwood furniture and seagrass mat kept the interior simple and uncluttered, meaning we didn't have to dodge heavy coffee tables or cupboards to reach the front door and slip into the heat-oppressive night.

A swim did sound good.

A swim beneath the cloudless star-scattered sky sounded almost as enticing as ripping off her bikini and pushing her against a tree.

But...Eleanor was right.

Anticipation was the best kind of foreplay.

Fine, I could be patient.

I think.

Tucking her into my side, I looked down her cleavage and the pinpricks of hard nipples beneath black Lycra. "I can see you're aroused, but how much?" Licking the shell of her ear, I asked, "How wet are you, Jinx?"

She shivered in my hold, but she didn't blush. We'd shared too many deliciously deviant things together to be embarrassed. "I'm getting wetter with every step. I will admit, I didn't think this through. A twenty-minute walk might just kill me." She blinked in the darkness. "Feel free to select any palm tree to have your wicked way with me."

I grinned. "Oh, you're not getting off that easy. You're the one who wanted to torture us. I'll oblige."

She moaned under her breath. "Tease."

"Witch." Chuckling, we fell into a familiar pace, leaving behind our home by Nirvana and stepping through the dark jungle where most nocturnal animals came awake and feasted on berries and moths. Most birds should be roosting by now but not our two parrots. The emerald flashes of their wings hinted they followed us, zipping through shadowy bushes and shooting toward the stars just because they could.

"You have a good day?" Eleanor asked.

My heart fisted. Who would've thought I'd be as enthralled to share my day with her as I was about having sex? Our domestication was as precious to me as entering Euphoria and having a night of freaky inhibition as cavewoman and Neanderthal.

That was one of our favourite fantasies, and we'd replayed it multiple times over the years.

I kissed her temple, unable to stop myself from squeezing her hip. "Yeah, good. Promising advances in a few areas. Peter Beck is keen to move to human trials."

"That's great." She smiled. "I'm glad. Oh, did you hear the news about Rapture? We've been awarded the best *Couple Retreat and Relationship Repair Award* from *Romance Tourism*."

I nodded. "I did. You should be proud."

"Not me." She shook her head, sending her long hair tickling my forearm wrapped around her waist. "You. Without your VR and *cinta*, we'd be just another place for doomed marriages to drag out their death in a therapist's office."

"You're the one who started that side of our business, Eleanor. Don't sell yourself short. The success of Rapture is all thanks to you."

"Maybe, but only because I was too selfish to have guests stay here." She waved her arm at our perfect solitude. At Pika and Skittles having an aerial battle above and the soft hoots of owls in the gloom. Sandstone-carved lanterns guided us with patches of stencilled light on the sand, and the only hint that we lived in a world where other humans existed was the faint laughter of a staff member enjoying his evening in the distance.

"I couldn't share this. Even though the goddess villas are empty and could've easily been rented out."

"I'm glad you suggested offsite. I'm glad Rapture is doing so well, and I'm also glad we don't have guests upon these shores anymore."

Rapture was the name of the three-island atoll I'd leased long term, just off the coast of Tahiti. We'd built matching villas there, designed guest areas, activities, and built a new Euphoria building.

Euphoria used to be how I made a shit ton of money renting out goddesses to men who wanted certain kicks. Now, it saved dysfunctional marriages.

Here, Euphoria had long since been transformed into an animal sanctuary, but on Rapture…a new chapter had begun. My virtual reality technology, coupled with the playrooms and aphrodisiac I'd tweaked from elixir, had been given a new purpose.

On Rapture, it helped unhappy couples duke out their problems, argue out their grievances, and then make up in spectacular fucking fashion.

Some couples, along with therapy and a weeklong stay—away

from the stress of life and meddling families—were able to focus on the nucleus of why they married each other and return home with a much happier marriage. Unfortunately, some couples, despite the immersion and help we gave them, couldn't let their guards down to even step into the virtual reality playground and divorced anyway.

And then there were the couples who enjoyed their fantasies so much, they purchased a home kit of VR sensors and a bottle of *cinta* to ensure sex remained fun within their relationship.

Thanks for the sales of VR and the outside use of my heavily copyrighted technology, yet another branch of our business had emerged.

The sensors that convinced a human's mind that what they heard, saw, felt, and tasted were as real as the life around them ensured such corporations like space travel, deep-sea diving, and everything in between had purchased kits for education.

Companies could now provide their staff with training before they ever had to put their life on the line.

Along with allowing tertiary places to bolster their classrooms with my device, I hired computer programmers to continue my crusade to stop all animal mistreatment in labs, slaughterhouses, and in meat, dairy, and egg industries.

With just a few sensors, people could now enter environments never open to the public before. They could step into a production plant of wheat and cereal. They could stand next to conveyor belts as toothbrushes were made from bamboo instead of plastic. And they could also witness the bone-chilling truth of mass animal cultivation and murder for consumerism.

They could feel the splash of a cow's blood as its throat was slit. They could smell the stench of defecation, knowing they were about to die. They could watch a thousand baby male chicks being tossed into a blender because they weren't valuable egg layers.

Before Eleanor, I wasn't proud of many things I'd done.

I bought women. I rented those women out. I felt no guilt because I only did to them what humans did to animals. I used our own laws of inequality to pad my wallet and justify my sins.

Now though, I was proud that in recent years, more and more people were waking up to the lies of corruption and the risk of their own health by eating the rancid panic of caged and miserable creatures. Things were changing. And I liked to think I had a small part in that.

I was also immensely proud of Eleanor.

Of her capacity for creating and running, not only a profitable company, but one that gave beneficial gifts toward people's happiness. I loved sharing ideas and brainstorming our next foray together.

I just loved her. In every way.

Every thought and twitch.

Every smile and snicker.

She owned me, heart and fucking soul.

"We should plan another visit one day." She rested her head on my arm as we continued strolling in the moonlight. "See if the weather is as perfect in the South Pacific as it is in Indonesia."

"Perhaps."

We walked in silence until the manicured jungle fell away and the beach appeared. Not a single breeze tonight. Not a ripple in the ocean. Stars bounced back in the mirror of black sea, a half-moon blindingly silver in two glittering locations.

Pika and Skittles stuck to the treeline while Eleanor and I slipped bare feet through silky warm sand and waded into the shallows.

We both sighed with contentment. Drinking in the stunning view, we thanked fate and everything magical that we'd found each other and were so fucking lucky to live in paradise.

"Wonder if Jess and Cal are looking at the sky right now." Eleanor tipped her head to the heavens, sending sheets of hair rippling down her back. My lust returned with a fist to my gut. Spinning her into me, I sank both hands into the strands at her nape and tugged her head back. "I don't fucking care what they're doing."

I kissed her hard.

Dropping one hand from her hair to press against her lower back, I joined our hips together.

She moaned as I thrust into her, showing her my hard-on, hinting that the time for talking was over.

Kissing her, I plucked her from the shallow sea and waded deeper.

I didn't stop until warm salt licked around my chest and threatened to make me buoyant.

Biting her lower lip, I let her go and shoved away her kimono until it floated on the surface before slowly waterlogging and sinking. With rough hands, I untied her bikini and let the scraps vanish. Unlike the time I'd tried to rescue her when she was high on elixir and I was knocking on death's door, there was nothing manic about this.

We'd fucked in the sea numerous times, and each time was a testament to our lust and the fact that even after years of marriage, we still hungered desperately for each other.

Her hands worked beneath the surface, ripping the Velcro holding my board shorts together and splaying them wide to dive her hand inside.

I hissed as her small fingers wrapped around my cock.

She pumped me all while I manhandled her legs to wrap around my hips, spreading her wide for me. I went to kiss her, but she angled her mouth away with a minx-like smile on her lips. "You know, that first week that I was captive here, I watched you swimming pretty much right where we are. I was spying on Jupiter, Neptune, and Calico as they drank cocktails and gossiped about you." Her eyes glowed. "Did you see me that night? You knew I was hiding…so I've always wondered if you saw me before coming to shore."

I grinned, running my right hand over the swell of her hip and dipping between her legs.

She gasped as I touched her, rubbing my finger over her clit before teasing inside her. "I wasn't swimming."

"No?" She groaned as I pushed my finger inside to the first knuckle. Withdrawing and pushing, I fucked her slowly, coaxing her body to become wet and slippery.

"I had my hand on my cock. I was fucking myself, all because I couldn't get you out of my goddamn mind." I speared two fingers inside her as far as they could go.

She spasmed in my hold. Her hand clutched at my cock. "Ah, God. So…you saw me. From out here?"

"Of course, I saw you. I saw you looking out to sea as if someone would come rescue you. I saw you sucking in air as if forcing yourself to stay brave. I saw you trying to figure out what was out at sea, not knowing it was me masturbating only a few metres away, wishing I was balls deep inside you." I inserted a third finger, spreading her, thrusting and taking.

"God, Sully." Her head fell back, giving me access to bite her delicious throat.

I ran my tongue along her skin, tasting salt and Eleanor.

Her fingers squeezed my cock, harder and faster, moving in time with my fingers inside her. "You bought me, and I hated you, yet I listened to those goddesses fantasising about you, and I wondered, just for a moment, what it would be like to touch you the way they wanted."

"They were never allowed."

"Just me."

"Just you. Only you. *Always* you."

She shivered as I kissed her again. We kissed and tongues tangled, and our hands punished each other, making whimpers fall from her and growls from me.

Breathing hard, she murmured, "Strange question but…why did you only buy women? You never bought any men to rent out."

I unsheathed my teeth and bit down, kissing and nipping her throat. "That *is* a strange fucking question."

She shrugged, breathy and trembling. "The only men on this island were your guards, trapping us."

"And you wanted some male prisoners because…why? You thought they might've helped get you free from me?" Jealousy rose in my chest, making me cruel. Ripping my fingers from her pussy, I grabbed her chin. "No one was going to save you from me, Jinx. I wanted you before you even arrived. You were never getting off this island, help or no help."

She let me tip her head sideways, dropping my hand to curl around her throat.

"I wasn't looking to escape…Well, I was, but that isn't why I asked."

"Why did you then?" I shuddered as her hand continued to pump my cock.

"Because I found myself jealous listening to those goddesses discussing you. I hated you, but the thought of anyone else touching you made my hate sizzle with fire. Looking back now, I'm glad there were no women guests. That the only competition I had were goddesses instead of high-powered, wealthy women with freakish fetishes come to rent a toyboy in Euphoria…come to seduce the *master* of those boy toys."

I struggled to smile, baring my teeth instead. "There's never been anyone else for me, Eleanor."

"I know…"

"You want to know why I only bought women? Why I only had a stable of goddesses instead of unwilling princes?" Knocking her hand off my cock, I grabbed the base and wrapped my arm tighter around her waist, angling us into position. "It's because the women who would be interested in renting them scared the fucking shit out of me. Men are monsters, without a shadow of a doubt, but women? Fuck, they eat monsters for lunch." I thrust up, filling my wife in one swift, possessive impale.

We both cried out.

Clawing at each other.

Kissing wetly, messily.

Thrusting in rhythm and letting our bodies fight, then sink into a fierce dance we knew so well.

When Eleanor and I fucked, we weren't gentle. Just because we loved each other didn't mean we didn't cause bruises. Our passion was dangerously explosive, and we lived for that mayhem when chasing a mutual orgasm that left us breathless, bitten, and bruised.

"What does that make me then?" She panted as I fucked her, swift and sharp.

"You?"

"I'm a woman."

"No, you're *the* woman."

"You're saying I'm worse than you? That I'm more dangerous than you?"

I grinned, thrusting up and hitting the top of her pussy. She shivered and moaned, her eyes becoming unfocused. "I'm saying you're dangerous in every way a woman is dangerous. You have the capacity to care and nurture, but you also have a gift of becoming cold-hearted and cutthroat. Men might be physically stronger, but women? Fuck, they can turn off their humanity just as easily. Better even."

"I'm not like that."

"Are you sure?" I kissed her.

Our tongues lashed and tangled.

Our thrusting bodies created tiny waves that spread out in ever-widening ripples, distorting the moon's reflection.

"What would you do if I were in trouble or hurt by someone? If someone threatened my life again?"

Eleanor stiffened even as I thrust into her. "I'd do whatever it took to keep you safe. *Whatever* it took." Her tone was icy and fierce, making my balls clench and heart skip.

"See, right there." I hugged her tight. "You're vicious... You just hide it. All women are vicious beneath their camouflage. Whatever men I could've rented out in Euphoria, let's face it; they wouldn't have survived as long as the goddesses. They would've broken."

"Because women are monsters?"

"Humans are monsters." I ran my thumb over her mouth.

"And I've found my perfect match in you. Enough talk of the past, hypothetical or real."

Eleanor smiled in the moonlight, sinking onto me, wrapping her legs tighter around me. "I love you, Sully Sinclair."

"I know." I stopped trying to be coherent and let my mind go. I allowed my blood to burn with the steady pressure of an orgasm. I fucked my wife as if she were my enemy, all while I worshipped her as if she could snuff out my sorry excuse of a life.

Because she could.

Capturing her mouth, I increased my speed until her breasts bounced in the sea, her cries turned louder, and the sound of her release echoed over the perfect midnight silence.

And I followed her.

I pumped inside and came in fisting waves of bliss.

I marked her as mine.

For always.

Chapter Three

"YOU GUYS COMING BACK anytime soon?" I asked.

Jess's voice sounded light-hearted and happier than I'd ever heard, skipping down the phone line in answer to my question. "Perhaps. Why? Do you miss us?"

"Tell Cal I much prefer my islands without him." Sully smirked from where he sat at his desk in his office. The apothecary cabinet that used to house multiple vials of elixir now held the less potent and deliciously enjoyable *cinta*—an aphrodisiac blended from orchid and who knew what else in Sully's laboratories.

Sunshine coated the tiled floor, Pika sat chirping beside Sully while trying to attack his keyboard, and Skittles was dozing on my shoulder, her little squeak-snores adorable in my ear.

It was yet another perfect day in our perfect paradise.

"Sully said he misses you, Jess, but Cal can stay in the Philippines."

"Bastard would cry if I never came back," Cal answered before Jess could. "He has no other friends."

"He has me." I grinned.

"Yeah, but you're a girl."

"Your point?" I raised an eyebrow.

"Married men need a trustworthy male friend to be able to complain about their wives. *Ouch.*" Cal chuckled. "Jess just hit me."

"You deserved it." She stole the phone back, still giggling. "We're thinking of coming back next week. But we should all come back here. The islands are stunning, and the diving is amazing."

"I've never been diving." I couldn't tear my eyes off Sully as he ran his fingers through his unruly dark hair, the ends once again sun-bleached from swimming in salt and living in sunshine.

How was that creature mine? How was his huge diamond on my finger and his marriage vows locked around my heart, binding us for eternity?

It honestly didn't seem possible. Especially considering I was sprawled, relaxed and happy, on the very same couch where Sully had sat and commanded I sit on his two fingers after force-feeding me libido-brutalising elixir when we first met.

Sully suddenly sat up, clicking the mouse and skimming something on his computer screen. Pika squawked and spied his opportunity to rip off a laptop key and toss it to the ground.

Sully looked up, catching my gaze. "Tell them we won't be here next week."

I sat up, interrupting Skittle's snooze. She yawned and fluffed up her feathers, tickling my neck. "Wait. Why?"

"What is it? What's going on?" Jess asked.

"Apparently, we won't be here next week," I said, still looking at Sully for more information.

He cocked his head, a half-smile on his face. The fact that he was smiling hinted the reason we weren't going to be here was a good thing. At least nothing urgent or unfortunate was dragging us away from our sanctuary.

"I'll call you later and fill you in." I stood from the couch and made my way to Sully's side.

Pika flew to my shoulder to head bump Skittles while Sully looped his arm around my hips, pulling me into him and typing one-handed with the other.

"Okay, be safe, you two." Jess blew kisses down the phone. "Speak to you soon."

"Can I speak to Sinclair super quick?" Cal asked, once again commandeering the phone from his wife. "Just so I don't have to worry about his ass?"

"Sure." Passing the phone to Sully, I mouthed, "It's Cal."

Sully rolled his eyes, taking the cell. "Yes, we're leaving. Yes, everything is fine. Yes, we'll be back in a few days. And no, there's nothing to panic about."

Cal muttered something that I couldn't hear, making Sully chuckle. "All you need to concern yourself with is keeping Jessica happy. Which for you might be hard, seeing as you're so disagreeable and all."

Cal's voice rose, but I still couldn't catch the male banter. Ever since Sully allowed the lines to blur from long-time employee and sometimes confidant to partners and best friends, he and Cal entered word wars that sometimes lasted for months with quips and slurs.

Jess and I stayed out of it.

After all, male bickering was a sport I had no business in understanding, just like Sully and Cal would never appreciate the silent looks Jess and I indulged in that could hold entire conversations and normally ended in knowing nods or conspiratorial giggles.

"We're going to England," Sully said, "to visit a friend."

Cal's questions fired back, and Sully answered good-naturedly, "I'm taking my wife and going to a ball, if you must know. A masquerade."

While Sully nodded and listened to whatever Cal regaled, I skimmed the email on his screen.

To: S.Sinclair@goddessisles.com
From J.H@HawksridgeHall.com
Subject: An invitation

Hello, Sullivan,

My wife and I are hosting a masquerade this weekend and would like to extend an invitation. I'm aware it's short notice, and I'm also aware this is not your scene. However, I'm still waiting to meet the new Mrs Sinclair, and I think it's high time we catch up in person instead of online, don't you?

Nila already has a gown in mind that would be perfect for Eleanor, and you are welcome to stay in any of our guest suites at Hawksridge Hall for however long you see fit.

Be a pleasure to host you.

Think about it.

The masquerade starts at 19:00 on Saturday.

Jethro

Sully laughed. "Yeah, yeah. We'll stay in touch. See ya." He hung up and squeezed me close. "So? Fancy going to a dance?"

"Where?"

"In an ancient castle where a bunch of scandalous events and history happened."

I smiled as Pika and Skittles fluttered from my shoulder to the bird feeder outside, chasing away the flock of resident sparrows and a cheeky squirrel. "Is it haunted?"

"Quite possibly." He nipped the side of my breast, pressing a kiss over the sting of his teeth. "But don't worry, I'll be there to protect you."

I wrapped my arm around his shoulders. "My hero."

"Been called many things, but never that." Sully grinned, showing the fine lines of happiness around his eyes and the etching of handsome weathering that only made him more distinguished. "I've been meaning to introduce you two. This way, we go, we play, we stay the night, and then we fly home."

"Okay." I nodded.

"You sure?" His blue eyes searched mine.

"Sounds fun."

"Okay then." Unwinding his arm from around my hips, he ducked to pluck the letter L from the floor where Pika had torn it off and clipped it back onto the keyboard. With swift, strong fingers, he confirmed our attendance.

We agreed to travel to England for a masquerade, hosted in a stuffy ancient castle in a drizzly cold country that was as far from our open-air island existence as possible.

I'd be lying if I said I wasn't excited to dance with my tuxedoed husband and enjoy meeting one of his oldest friends, but…I would miss Goddess Isles. I'd miss Pika and Skittles. I'd miss our utopia.

My gaze fell on the apothecary cabinet, and an idea sprang to mind.

And suddenly, I didn't feel quite so homesick.

Because I had a plan.

An extra little something that I would pack in my suitcase to ensure we had a way to escape if we needed to.

Sullivan

Chapter Four

"WHAT DO I CALL him?" Eleanor asked, her voice pitched with nerves. "Do I bow? What about his wife? Do I curtsy?"

"They aren't royalty, Jinx." I watched the English countryside streak past as we drove from the airport to Buckinghamshire. "At least, I don't think they are."

I'd never actually checked.

When I received that first email from a resident psychiatrist at an English hospital we donated to, claiming to have a teenage boy with behavioural issues that were amplified depending on who was in the room with him, I'd agreed to personally find a mix of drugs to help.

Originally, I'd wondered if he was schizophrenic, but after professional curiosity led to me phoning the teenager in question and ending up having a conversation that made my scientific brain race with a quest to understand, I realised Jethro's condition was far more interesting than schizophrenia.

I hadn't long been in charge of Sinclair and Sinclair Group— barely out of my teens myself—so I took a personal interest in Jethro's case, purely because beneath his shields and snarls, I heard what I saw in all trapped animals: the cry for help and the broken faith not to believe in hope.

When we'd spoken, he'd originally been stiff and aristocratically cold, yet the more we talked, the more he relaxed to the point he was analysing himself, just as I was, instead of having his hackles up about his 'disease'.

It was never a disease.

Not in the physical sense, at least. Jethro Hawk had an affliction that I suffered with to a much lesser degree. The same reason I'd begun my hunt and rampage against all animal testers and abusers.

A reason that I was able to shut off and buy women for my own means. And a reason that drove Jethro into a dark, miserable place where he almost killed the very woman he fell in love with.

"It's very pretty here," Eleanor murmured beside me. Her fingers pressed against the window as quaint brick walls, tiny country lanes, and patchwork fields skimmed past.

Not a hint of an ocean.

Not a single palm tree or parrot.

My skin itched beneath my suit, already wanting to turn around and return to Indonesia. But…I'd agreed to attend, and I wanted to see the change in Jethro now he had two kids as well as a wife.

Were they as much a cure as she was?

"Are you tired?" I asked gently, letting the driver navigate the fork up ahead that took us deeper into the English countryside.

"Not really. I slept on the plane. You?"

I'd worked most of the trip, but thanks to the first-class suite we'd shared—complete with a queen-sized bed and private bathroom—I was rested enough to attend a ball tonight.

"I'm good. We have a few hours before the other guests arrive. Jethro said he's arranged a room for us, and his staff know we're coming."

"So…he won't be there to start with?"

"I'm guessing he'll be mentally preparing for a night of people."

Her eyebrows rose. "Not a fan of society either?"

I smirked. "Not at all. If he could live on an island like we do, I have no doubt he'd leap at the chance."

"I think most people would."

I grabbed her hand and kissed her knuckles as the car slipped beneath the gatehouse with a huge crest of hawks fighting over something. An impressive seal for an ancient ruthless family.

"Well, who needs an ocean for a wall when you have a stone one?" I eyed up the entrance, the stone fortress snaking off up a hill and down a valley. The long driveway climbed through meadows and woodlands, weaving left and right, hinting that the estate we'd arrived at went on for miles and miles.

"This is where they live?" Eleanor gasped as a herd of deer bounded through the shrubbery, scampering off in a flash of perfect choreographed leaps. "It's stunning."

I nodded. I'd never visited Hawksridge Hall, but I had researched Jethro when our medical conversations turned friendlier. I had no trust when it came to people, and research was always a great way of arming yourself with everything you needed so you weren't surprised when they betrayed you.

I'd seen the rumours of debts and contracts over one house and another. I'd heard the gossip about diamond collars and beheadings. And I'd seen the photos of their exclusive castle that put any king or queen's residence to shame.

"Would you rather a beach or brocade?" I asked, narrowing my eyes at my wife. "I can build you a fancier villa than the one we share with sugar gliders and Komodo dragons, you know. Just say the word, and you can live in a palace."

She rolled her eyes, pinning me with a look that called me stupid even if she didn't say it out loud. "Do I look like I want brocade?"

"Sitting in this car, surrounded by expensive upholstery, you look positively trapped." I flinched, seeing the truth of such a sentence. I'd never seen Eleanor in a city environment when we first met. I'd dragged her to my shores and trapped her on my islands and fallen in love with her all while she was dressed in bikinis instead of ball gowns, but the truth was…the wildness inside her—the sun glowing from her skin, the oceans swirling in her grey gaze, and the sand still sparkling in her hair—hinted that she'd always been unfit for cookie-cutter houses and concrete office blocks.

That was probably why she'd had a love of travelling…so she could find the place where she fit in.

Thank fucking God, it was with me.

Undoing her seatbelt and dragging her onto my lap, I brought her mouth to mine just as we crested the hill. I kissed her softly, our lips moving in a well-known dance even as our eyes stayed locked on the massive monolithic hall that took up the entire horizon.

Turrets and lattice grass wound through stone bricks, hundreds of windows, thousands of arches, gothic downpipes, and a roof designed like an intricate puzzle.

We pulled apart as the car drove around the huge water fountain and parked at the bottom of sweeping stairs leading to a medieval wooden door that promised pain and power the moment you stepped over its threshold. Every inch of this place from the groomed gravel, immaculately pruned gardens, and hulking hall ensured visitors were well aware that ordinary men didn't live here.

Monsters did.

Eleanor pulled away, her eyes wide as a butler appeared, opening the massive door and standing prim and proper as he waited for us to ascend. "Suddenly, I really, really miss Goddess Isles."

I ran my fingers through her hair, letting her climb off my lap as our driver came to open our door. "We can turn around if you want."

She shook her head. "No, you're here to see a friend." Flashing me a smile, she added, "And besides, I've never spent a night in an ancient hall before. It'll be fun."

"Fun or haunted."

"If there are ghosts in there, they'd better stay far away until we leave."

A black crow flew past as we climbed from the car, its midnight wings glistening with a wicked sharp beak that could kill any rodent or prey it spied. My mind instantly went to Pika and Skittles. They'd been pissed we'd left them behind, but at least, they wouldn't become lunch.

"Welcome, Mr and Mrs Sinclair." The butler descended a few steps, his youngish face stern but polite. He kept his brown stare on the driver as he lifted out our small amount of luggage. Just one bag between Eleanor and myself. We didn't plan to stay long, and Jethro had assured me that the masquerade attire for tonight had been taken care of.

The butler took the bag, climbing up the huge staircase. "Follow me, please. I will escort you to your room. Mr and Mrs Hawk are otherwise indisposed this afternoon but look forward to seeing you at the ball tonight."

I nodded. "Thank you."

Eleanor stayed quiet beside me as we followed the butler out of the weak English sun and into the oppressive majesty of Hawksridge Hall. The stone flagons on the floor and the bolts of tapestries hanging from the high ceiling all spoke of lineages, history, and blood-soaked secrets.

The hall was warm, which I found surprising, considering the age of such a place that still favoured antiquated methods instead of modern conveniences, and the deeper we travelled into the impressive mansion, the more I noticed primeval ideologies were slowly being replaced with the aura of a family home.

The suit of armour, polished and threatening at the end of the carpeted corridor had a stuffed purple elephant at its feet. The paintings of past Hawk ancestors in their stuffy suits and dresses had the faintest of scribbles from a child's sneaky crayon.

Sound echoed and muffled in equal measure the deeper we travelled into the giant homestead, thick rich carpets sat like islands on top of slate tile and stone.

Everyone stayed silent as we climbed a staircase that swept up with ornate carved banisters and gold carpet stitched with the Hawk emblem.

"This way, please." The butler continued down yet another corridor, past floor-to-ceiling windows overlooking an impressive orchard and manicured hedgerow maze, past wooden doors and nooks with wingbacks and stained-glass lamps to read by. At the end of the long corridor, the butler stopped and opened another large door, stepping aside with a stiff bow. "Your quarters for the duration of your stay at Hawksridge."

Eleanor smiled politely, slipping past him, gasping at the splendour.

"Thank you." I shook the man's hand as he placed our bag on the floor and scooted from the room. With a tight smile, he shut the door, leaving Eleanor and me alone in a bedroom almost the same size as our entire villa back on *Batari*.

"Wow." Eleanor drifted forward. We'd been given a room along the side of the huge hall, granting us impressive quarters.

A small kitchenette was tucked by the entrance, a doorway led to a luxurious black marble bathroom and a claw-foot tub big enough for four waited for use. Pacing deeper into the space, I skimmed the maroon velvet sitting area complete with chaise lounge down the east end, a small library with towering bookcases filled with classics in the middle, and a four-poster bed with a mattress you needed a ladder to climb into waited with fresh white sheets and rich crimson coverlets toward the west.

The scent of jasmine wafted in the space, and what was left of the afternoon sun spilled into the entire length of the room, thanks to the ten huge windows giving us a view of the meadows toward the stone stables in the distance.

Eleanor stopped by one of the large windows, drinking in the view. "Well, it's not the sea, but the vista is spectacular."

I wrapped my arms around her from behind, pulling her close. "It's impressive."

"Wonder if the stables are used or—" Her hand swooped up, pointing at a sudden movement within the willows beyond. "Horses."

Three horses, to be exact.

Two adults and one child cantered from the treeline, all competent and carefree. The man rode a black horse, leading the way, a woman followed on a dapple grey with a small toddler sitting in front of her, and a tiny boy charged ahead on a fat little pony.

I smiled. "I'm guessing that's our host and hostess."

"The Hawks?" Eleanor tracked them as the family swept up the meadow and over the ridge beyond in a flurry of hooves. "They ride?"

"I think Jethro even plays polo. While we were trialling certain drugs, he admitted that being on horseback was the only relief he could find before his wife came along."

"How did they meet?" Eleanor twisted in my embrace, standing on her tiptoes to kiss me. "Do they have a story like ours? A kidnapping turned fairy-tale? Or perhaps an arranged marriage turned into love? Or even a forbidden romance where they had to overcome so many things?"

I smirked, kissing her back. I'd never asked Jethro point-blank about the rumours I'd read online. After all, I had my own fair share of gossip and slander painting me as a murderer and ruthless bastard. And where rumours existed, truth was never far away.

Therefore, the whispers surrounding the firstborn Hawk son had a grain of honesty.

"They say that Jethro was given Nila as a present on his birthday."

Eleanor wrinkled her nose. "She's a person, not a gift."

"Oh, it wasn't a gift. More like a test." I let Eleanor go and strode toward the garment bags waiting to be unzipped on the back of the couch. "If she's wearing a diamond collar tonight, I'm guessing there's more truth to the tale than I thought."

"What tale? What collar?" Eleanor came up beside me, staying close as I unzipped the largest of the bags.

"Tale of debts, diamonds, and death." Pushing aside the black covering, I revealed a ball gown. And not just any ball gown...a dress fit for the most regal of queens.

"Oh, my God." Eleanor reached out to touch the exquisite creation. "Where on earth did this come from? I've never seen anything so...*gorgeous*."

"Jethro's wife is a seamstress." I held up the hanger, slipping off the rest of the garment bag.

I grew hard the longer I stared.

My lust ignited just imagining Eleanor in this dress. She wouldn't just be irresistible to me; she'd be the most stunning creature at the masquerade.

And she's mine.

Plucking a matching mask from the bag, she murmured, "She isn't just a seamstress; she's a magician."

"She's made it impossible for me to keep my hands to myself tonight." I swallowed back a growl full of possession and need. "If any other man looks at you, I can't promise I won't drag you into the nearest closet and tear that thing off you."

She fluttered her eyelashes. "I doubt there are closets in this place, my love. More like dungeons."

"A dungeon will do."

"You've got that look in your eyes again."

"What look?"

"The one that says you own me and want to show me in every explicit detail how much."

I licked my lips. "Do you have a problem with that?"

"No problem." She laughed. "In fact, I'll keep a lookout for a dungeon, just so you can have your wicked way with me."

I grinned. "And that is why I love you, Eleanor Jinx Sinclair. You're as obsessed as I am."

"Forever obsessed." She raked her hands through my hair, pulling me down for a vicious kiss.

Grabbing her around the waist, I dragged her toward the bathroom. I needed her naked. Now. "Guess we better get ready for the ball, wife. After all, the sooner we mingle, the sooner we can be alone."

Chapter Five

THE HEAVY WEIGHT OF my ball gown swished and clung to me.

Every layer and detail gave me power and mystery, ensuring I became unrecognisable. My mask hid my forehead and eyes, the cut so perfect it looked as if it was a part of me and not a disguise.

To be honest, I felt freer than I'd ever been and also terribly lost. I liked the sensation of wearing a dress designed for a princess, but I also scrambled to remember the simple girl within me. The girl who could spend an entire week wearing different coloured gemstone bikinis and nothing else. The girl who drank coconut water straight from the nut and frequently had dirt under her fingernails from helping in the vegetable gardens on *Lebah.*

As much as Sully's wealth allowed us to live a life of utmost luxury, we were simple in our tastes. The money we spent was on animal welfare, medicine, and rehoming.

As long as we were safe on our island together, that was all we ever needed.

And this? This gown made me look as if I'd stepped from one Eden into another. One full of decadence and danger.

Sully strode beside me, his arm looped with mine, his back straight beneath the smoky grey tux that shimmered silver in lamplight and unforgiving metallic in the darkness. I studied him out of the corner of my eye. His mask covered his entire head, leaving only his nose and jaw exposed. His blue eyes glowed behind the grey disguise, harsh and delicious.

White beads decorated where his eyebrows would be, twining in a complex design up and over his skull, leading to two horns that were ridged like a goat's.

He could be a devil or a demigod…or both.

He was the most magnificent man I'd ever seen, and…*he's mine.*

As we glided past the windows, opaque and reflecting like mirrors now that night-time had fallen, I caught glimpses of myself. I saw a delectable woman on his arm that was every bit as impressive and imposing as he.

My gown matched Sully's tux in infinitesimal ways. The bottom of my skirts was smoky grey—as if I'd stepped in clouds and hadn't fully shed their cloying colour—but beyond that…I was iridescent.

A snakeskin pattern etched the fabric, growing from faint lines into bold patterns the higher up the bodice it went. From my hips to my shoulders, the fabric was almost sheer, allowing opalescent scales to hint at my flesh beneath. Two fabric trains fell from my shoulder blades, adding to the swatches of material following me down the sweeping staircase toward the murmur of voices and the crush of crowds below.

As we'd prepared for the masq, we'd heard more and more guests arrive. The crunch of gravel as limousines pulled up and deposited their partygoers, and the occasional roar of a helicopter landing on the grounds.

Once again, a window refracted my appearance, revealing that my dress might be based on a snake's sinuous, silky poison but also garnered inspiration from other creatures too.

The long gloves I wore went up my biceps, intricately detailed with beadwork in the shape of bees and butterflies. Stitched over the iridescent snakeskin fabric were the tiniest of seashells and within the smoky grey swirling around my feet were the starched lace embellishments in the shape of feathers and fronds.

My mask had matching horns to Sully's, only on a smaller scale, along with diamonds over my brow and along my cheekbones.

The entire ensemble was a mismatch of reptilian, avian, sea life, and ground dwellers. All animal themed in high-end couture.

Reaching the bottom of the staircase, I clung to Sully's arm as we braced ourselves and headed toward the hum of voices.

Flutters of my orgasm that Sully had given me in our shared shower continued to tease between my legs.

It'd taken two attempts to get dressed, thanks to Sully's insatiable desire the moment I'd slipped into the gown.

We didn't need to talk to know that tonight would be enjoyable but also a struggle to mingle with so many strangers. As long as Sully stayed close by, I would be content to smile and chat, despite missing the serenity of our shores.

Brushing past a few couples, we stepped into the giant ballroom.

It took my breath away.

Pillars and tumbling velvet curtains. Wainscoting and plasterwork ceilings. Six ginormous chandeliers drenched gowned and tuxedoed guests in fragmenting rainbows.

The room was crowded but not overly so, all attention upon the small podium where a band had paused in their playing. A man in a black tux with a black mask stood beside a woman in a raven and swan dress, black feathers blending into white with a half-mask covering one eye.

They spoke, but we were too far away to hear exactly what was said. However, Sully nuzzled my nose, murmuring, "That's him. Jethro and his wife. See her necklace?"

I nodded. How could I miss the huge diamond collar around her throat? "She's beautiful."

Sully grunted, his eyes not on our hosts but the head of his security, Radcliffe.

Radcliffe and a few of his team from Quietus—his old mercenary firm—now lived on Goddess Isles with us and protected whatever needed protecting. He'd travelled with us, staying discreet and unseen.

Radcliffe nodded once in our direction, spoke into his cuff to the rest of his team, and faded back into the crowd.

A round of applause sounded along with a roar of laughter, dragging my attention to a man in a white tux standing beside a woman in a gorgeous gown sitting in a wheelchair.

And then the speech was over, and the Hawks vanished from the stage. The band struck up a romantic, soulful serenade, and the party began.

"Want to dance, my lovely goddess?" Sully asked, turning to me with a graceful bow.

I placed my hand in his. "I can't dance, but if it's an excuse to touch you, then definitely."

He grinned, pulling me through the crowd to the dance floor where other couples had fallen into a waltz.

I'd never ballroom danced in my life. "Eh, what do I do?"

Sully gathered me close, angling me correctly and spreading my arm out with his. "Just follow my lead. I don't exactly know what I'm doing either but just follow the music. Who cares about the proper steps."

Biting my lip, I allowed him to glide me forward and back, my dress swaying and train pooling by my feet as we swept around the floor.

To start with, self-consciousness kept me highly aware of other more talented couples. But then the song changed to a more passionate rendition, and masked men clutched their women closer, spun faster, encouraging lust to mingle within the finery of decorum.

My own need struck a sizzling match.

Sully's touch went from comforting and familiar to laced with that heady electricity that always got us into trouble. My breath came quicker as I did my best to ignore the crackling chemistry and copy others, focusing on mastering my dancing instead of pouncing on my gorgeous husband.

Unfortunately, Sully felt it too. Nuzzling his nose against my throat, he sent another scattering of fireworks through my blood. "You're flushed, my love. Is it from my dancing or perhaps something else?"

I moaned.

I couldn't help it.

My breasts grew heavy. My core liquefied. My fingernails dug into him as I fought rapidly building desire. Sully had always triggered my primordial nature. From the moment we'd met, our bond had transcended conversation and even emotional connection. It was raw and violent and—

"I need you, Sully," I breathed. "Dancing was a bad idea."

He gripped me hard, swaying me to the beat. With him pressed so close, I took liberties that would guarantee retribution. My hand snaked from his waist and around his muscular thigh. My gown blocked others from seeing as I wrapped my fingers around his impressive erection.

He jerked. His quick gasp making me wet and tingly.

"Jinx..." His growl wrenched my head up.

His blue eyes glowed like the Java Sea as he cupped my cheek and ran his thumb over my mouth. His touch instantly ignited a thousand kisses and a million touches we'd shared over the years.

And I lost myself to him.

Another song began, and our bodies melted into each other. My fingers stroked him through his silky tux trousers. He clawed at my back and cupped my chin with dominance. His head came down, mine tipped back, and our lips connected without any care of people watching.

My hair had been left loose, draping down my back where Sully tangled his fingers within the strands and pulled.

I forgot how to breathe as he kissed me deeper. Our masks grazed each other's, goosebumps covered me beneath glistening snake scales, and I forgot that we weren't free to do whatever we wanted.

Living on an island meant we had privacy to indulge in our lust whenever the hell we wanted. If Sully wanted me over his desk, he could. If he wanted me when walking back to Nirvana, we could be as loud and as wild as needed.

I hated clothing.

I hated that I couldn't climb him right now and have him plunge inside me.

"God, Sully." I moaned into our kiss as he guided me around the perimeter of the dance floor. Our lips nipped and connected. Our blood crackled for more. Our tempers ignited to be alone.

While we danced, our hands roamed.

Our tongues tangled.

Our hearts possessed each other.

As another song began, we were once again on an island. Only this time, we were in a sea of strangers instead of the wide-open ocean.

"Fuck, I want you," he groaned into my mouth as we completed another circuit, moved to another song, and allowed the music to fully corrupt us.

I rubbed myself against him, shivering with need. "Do you think anyone would miss us if we went to find that dungeon?" I licked at his mouth as he kissed me hard. "I need you inside me."

"Fucking hell—" His kiss turned into a meal, tasting me, chasing my tongue and biting my bottom lip as I submitted. His large hand splayed on my lower back, wedging my hips against his as he ground himself indecently into my gown.

Panting, he pulled away and looked down my chest, his gaze hot and wild. "I can practically see your nipples through that dress. If we find somewhere to fuck, I can't guarantee it will be intact afterward."

I shuddered with his threat. "I'm okay with that."

"Don't think our hostess will be."

"It's her fault that I can't keep my hands off you."

He smirked. "Pretty sure it's *me* who can't keep my hands off you."

I cupped him again, squeezing his hot length. "We share the same affliction."

Sully's throat rippled as he swallowed down a snarl and pushed my hand away. "Don't push me, Eleanor. I'm seconds away from—"

"Can I cut in?" a smooth English voice said.

Sully froze. Anger flashed in his eyes as he arched his head over his shoulder. His shoulders braced to ensure whoever asked for a dance with me fully understood who I belonged to, only for him to relax and a strained chuckle to slip through his lips. "Jethro. Hello."

Pushing me to his side and wrapping his arm around me, Sully ran a hand over his jaw as if doing his best to shed our unsatisfied desire. "You don't have the best timing, but it's nice to see you." He held out his hand. "Thanks for the invite."

Jethro stood stoic, his head with its black mask tilting to the side. He studied us for a few seconds before a smirk lifted his lips. "If you're contemplating where the nearest empty room is, I can assist you." He shook Sully's hand. "I must warn you, though, Hawksridge has a habit of getting you lost if you don't know your way around. And I fear you might not return if you leave. Besides." He laughed under his breath. "They do say anticipation is the best kind of foreplay."

Sully chuckled. "Not hiding your tricks these days, I see."

"Hard to ignore when you're broadcasting your wants so loudly. You have a one track mind, my friend. Sex instead of enjoying my exclusive masquerade. I'd be offended if I wasn't so amused."

"*Jethro.*" A woman appeared by his side, swatting his arm. "What's gotten into you? You know you shouldn't pry into—"

"Relax, Nila." Jethro released Sully's hand. "He knows what I'm capable of. He knows most things about me."

"And it seems you know me. I'll have to remember to protect my thoughts around you. What did we agree on in our second drug trial? Something about humming a nonsense song to prevent you from—"

"I'm afraid I've evolved since then." Jethro laughed again, his tone dark but friendly. "You're at my mercy while in my hall."

"Or you're at mine." Sully grinned. "Seeing as you just complained my thoughts are rather loud. I could make your life a living hell."

"They're so loud, you're giving me the urge to vanish with my wife and find a dark corner."

"Kite!" The woman next to Jethro swatted him again.

Sully chuckled louder before bowing. "Hello, Mrs Hawk. Stunning as always." Before Nila could respond, Sully turned his attention back to his friend. "You were wrong, by the way." He bared his teeth. "We weren't thinking about finding an empty room, more like a dungeon. I'm sure you have a few of those beneath this castle."

Jethro paled slightly before mirroring Sully's grin. "Of course. Complete with manacles and a rack. However, I wouldn't recommend either. Not nearly as fun as advertised."

"I give up." Nila threw her hands in the air. "Honestly."

Sully let out a bark of laughter. "If I care to believe the rumours, old friend, I'd wager you know many methods of torture."

Jethro once again stilled before he shed his tension with a smile. "Rumours exist for both of us, don't they, Sullivan?"

"They do indeed." The two men studied each other before they conceded whatever competition they'd shared. "Good to see you. It's been too long."

"I agree." Jethro smiled at me. "And that's why I'm pissed you were thinking of leaving the masquerade so soon."

"I blame your wife for that." Sully chuckled. "The dress is very…enticing, Mrs Hawk."

"Call me Nila, please." Jethro's wife smiled.

"He's right, Needle. His appreciation of your work is…loud." Jethro laughed as the woman beside him pinched his waist.

"Behave, Jet. I swear to God."

"It's fine, Nila," Sully said. "He's only trying to embarrass me and my wife."

"I'm trying to aid you and your wife in a situation you are both in the midst of. But I'm going to be selfish and ask that you restrain yourselves so we can enjoy your company before you disappear."

What the hell is going on?

I couldn't make sense of this.

Who *was* this man?

And why did Sully act as if speaking to a clairvoyant wasn't a big deal. "It seems being drug-free has enabled an even greater sensory ability." Sully narrowed his eyes behind his mask. "It would be intriguing to test you again, Jethro. See where your skills lie, now that you're a happily married family man."

"Perhaps." With another smirk, Jethro turned his focus on me, changing the subject as if he had no intention of being Sully's test subject. "I'm sorry for my behaviour, Ms. Grace. It's rare for me to be able to share my true self, and I apologise if I upset you."

Before I had time to speak, Sully muttered, "It's Eleanor Sinclair. Not Grace. Not anymore."

"Of course. How clumsy of me." Jethro waited until I put my gloved hand in his, then he kissed my knuckles. His thumb ran over the bumps of my diamond rings that had been fashioned by his jewellers with Hawk diamonds. "You are, I must say, perfect for him."

I tugged my hand back, slightly unnerved by whatever abilities he possessed. "We've just met, so I'm not sure how you can say that but…thank you."

"I feel like I know you well." His bronze eyes twinkled. "I'm glad you found each other. And I'm glad the clothes my wife made fit so well and have my friend's approval."

Nila rolled her eyes, only half her pretty face obscured by her mask. Her dark hair was tied back, and the black and white feathers on her gown rippled with air eddies as couples danced past.

"Hi, Eleanor, I'm Nila. Ignore my husband." She held out her gloved hand. "Pleasure to meet you."

I nodded, shaking hers gently. "Likewise."

She grinned as two tiny children bolted past, ducking around ladies' skirts and racing past men's legs. "And those two hurricanes are our children."

Jethro chuckled as the kids vanished into the throng. "Kes and Emma. You'll meet them later."

Sully cocked his head, studying his friend. "Family life truly agrees with you, Jet."

"It does. No drug can compare." He sighed, his humour fading a little. "I'm sure I'll pay for this little soirée, but I thought it was time to begin introducing Emma and Kes to society. Prove to the tabloids and conspiracy theorists that whatever rumours plague Hawksridge are no more."

"Fair enough." Sully gathered me close, tucking me into his side. "So far, the ball seems like a success."

"It's an overly glorified business convention, really," Jethro said. "I invited you to catch up, but it's also a good time to make new contacts for your business. Especially the new islands in the South Pacific. Rapture, was it?"

"Correct." Sully nodded. "We're thinking about a visit there ourselves, actually. You and your family are welcome to come."

"Maybe." Jethro smiled. "For now, how about I introduce you around? You'd be doing me a favour by taking some of the attention off me. I can feel it a little too keenly."

Sully threw me a look. "I'm happy to come, but I don't particularly want to leave Eleanor."

"By all means, bring her—"

"Oh, don't you worry about her," Nila said. "She'll be bored while you talk business. I'll happily keep her entertained." Coming closer, Nila murmured, "I'm sure you have questions about my strange husband. And I can give you a tour if you'd like? Show you the gardens or the greenhouses. Maybe the stables?"

"Oh, that's kind." My unwillingness to leave Sully vanished. Our chemistry faded in preparation of being apart. I looked at Sully, my heart glowing as he nodded gently.

"I won't be long. I'll come find you after." His eyes heated with sinful promises.

"Okay." Smiling at Nila, I added, "I'd love to see your horses. We saw you riding this afternoon."

Nila beamed. "The stables it is. I should've offered that option first, seeing as I've heard about your fondness for animals." She motioned toward my snakeskin dress. "That was designed in a collection a year or so ago, but I figured it was perfect for you. In hindsight, I should've embellished it with more creatures. There truly are unlimited patterns you can pull from nature." She eyed my dress with critique rather than satisfaction. Annoyance clouded her gaze, then inspiration glowed bright. "Oh! I could do an entire collection based on the attributes of hunter and prey! I could design fangs out of wire and—"

"Needle, stop." Jethro chuckled. "We have friends to entertain, not new wardrobes to create."

Nila nudged him with her shoulder. "I can do both at once."

"Don't listen to her." Jethro looked at Sully, then me. "If you let her discuss clothing, you'll find yourself sitting in her sewing room while she sketches until tomorrow."

Taking Sully's elbow, Jethro bowed at me and his wife. "On that note, we'll see you two ladies in a bit. Don't get up to mischief."

Nila fluttered her eyelashes. "But I like mischief."

"Yes well, our intention tonight is to squash the rumours, not to create more by making me chase after you to ensure you behave."

Nila laughed, glancing at Sully. "See what I have to live with? He can do whatever he wants, but me? No way. Do you threaten your wife on a daily basis like he does?"

"I'd say almost hourly, actually," I said before Sully could. "Then again, I issue my own just as often."

Nila laughed harder. "I'd like to hear these threats." Stepping back, she opened her arm in invitation. "You can give me some pointers. Shall we? A quiet walk to the stables will be a perfect time for gossip."

Sully groaned. "Jethro, I'm happy your wife provides you with the emotional stability you need, but I'm not so keen on her corrupting mine."

"If anyone is doing the corrupting, it will be your wife, not mine." Jethro grinned. "Come on. Let me introduce you to our guests." Kissing Nila, he broke away from our group, giving Sully privacy to kiss me goodbye.

His kiss was swift and strict. A dominant reminder that we belonged together, and that he'd come find me soon. "I won't be long. Stay safe, Jinx."

I kissed him back. "You too."

Nila took my hand and dragged me the other way as Sully followed Jethro into the crowd.

Sullivan

Chapter Six

"SO HOW EXACTLY DID you get that stunning creature to fall in love with you?"

I punched Jethro in the arm as we left the ballroom and slipped into a quieter dayroom. "You saying I'm not lovable?"

"I'm saying you don't exactly let down your guard." My old friend grinned. "What's it been, Sully? Over a decade of friendship and you've never once been involved."

"Too busy."

"No excuse." He crossed his arms.

"You can't talk. You never had anything serious until Nila."

"That's because I couldn't get close to anyone but my brother Kes." He flinched as if his brother's death was still new and bleeding. In a way, it was. No matter how many years passed, I doubted Jethro would get over his middle brother's death. He didn't care about his younger brother's demise, mainly because he deserved it. Just like his father's end was justified.

Just like my own family deserved to be put down.

Wonder what he'd say if I told him what I'd done to my brother. How I'd broken his mind before Eleanor ended his body? How I celebrated his passing instead of mourned?

"How's that going, by the way?" I spied a bar trolley and helped myself to the high-end cognac in the decanter. Pouring myself a tumbler, I passed one to Jethro.

He nodded as he accepted and took a sip. "As I said in our conversations, I can't explain it." He shrugged. "To start with, I had too many influences over me. But the closer Nila and I grew together, the more I couldn't deny that I found peace with her. Peace that was so much more effective than any chemical."

"I'm glad." I sipped the rich liquor. "Put me out of a job."

"I heard a rumour you're being nominated for a Nobel Peace Prize for the drug that stopped that brewing pandemic."

I scratched my jaw, wishing I could remove my mask but accepting the masquerade ritual. "It wasn't anything special. We just targeted the virus strain and tested it with already known antibodies, then we mutated it for the current virus. It wasn't rocket science."

"To you, perhaps." Jethro finished his drink, placing the tumbler on a side table. "And I'm fully aware you've changed the subject. You forget what I am, Sinclair. I know it's been an age since we saw each other in person, but I remember how you felt back then, and it's entirely different to how you feel now."

If I didn't know and understand Jethro's condition, I would eye him with suspicion for such a comment. Only thing was, I'd categorically, scientifically proven that what Jethro sensed wasn't bullshit but some heightened sense of instinct that not all humans had tapped into.

In his case, he couldn't switch it off.

"How did I feel back then?" I finished my drink, looking over my shoulder to where music drifted from the ballroom. Was Eleanor safe? I knew Radcliffe would follow her and keep her protected while away from me but I had to admit, I fucking hated being apart from her.

"You were...cold." Jethro paced by the fireplace. "Analytical. No hint of feeling just...calculations. A brain that overruled any emotion and left you unexcited about anything and pissed off at everything."

"Sounds about right."

"But now, you——" He cocked his head, staring at me. "You're anxious right now because you're away from her, but when she was beside you——" He chuckled. "You were a horny bastard as well as possessive and protective. You were happy."

"Having a wife will do that to a man."

"No, having the perfect wife will do that." Jethro cleared his throat. "Nila saved me as surely as you saved me in my younger years. You helped deaden me to things I couldn't control, and she helped me rise above it." He cleared his throat. "I want to get to know Eleanor, Sullivan. You'll stay for breakfast tomorrow? Just the four of us?"

I nodded. "Of course."

"And perhaps she can answer my question."

"What question?"

"The one I asked earlier. How you conned her into falling in love with you." He laughed as I scowled.

"You really want to know?" I smirked, testing the truth on my tongue. No one outside of Cal and Jess and my loyal staff knew about my purchase of Eleanor. Apart from that Q bastard who'd threatened me the week or so before our wedding, of course.

Something like that should remain a secret, but Jethro had his own, and...I trusted him.

"I bought her." I kept a careful eye on him. "I bought her, trapped her, and knew instantly that she was mine. Luckily for me, she felt the same way."

"How quickly did you free her?"

"When my brother came to kill her."

Jethro's jaw stiffened, his mask hiding the rest of his expression. "I'm assuming, because Eleanor is still alive, that he failed in that quest?"

"He did."

He studied me for an unnerving second before nodding. In that one stare, I was almost sure he knew that Drake was dead and that I was glad of it.

"We have lots to catch up on, it seems." He guided me from the room. "At breakfast, we will have privacy. For now, let me introduce you to a man who I think can deliver some extra toys for your guests on Rapture."

"Toys?"

"Yachts. A Mr Elder Prest comes highly recommended."

"You getting into the sailing business yourself, Hawk?" I followed him, past the ballroom and down the corridor.

"Perhaps."

A tuxedoed gentleman swept from a morning room, almost colliding with us. Jethro went to introduce us, but I guessed this was the man he'd mentioned. He had the impatience of someone wanting to be elsewhere, rather than conversing with potential clients.

Like me.

"Mr Prest, I presume."

He eyed me, his mask hiding his nationality and features. "You presume correctly. And you are?" His accent was faint but reminded me of a Eurasian girl I'd bought once who lived half her life with her father in Japan and half with her mother in the States—before I'd imprisoned her, of course.

I swallowed back the memory. That wasn't who I was anymore. I hadn't been that man for a very long time. Jethro shifted beside me, hinting that perhaps the flush of memory from my past had done more than just infected my mind but my outward appearance too.

I had a habit of smiling sharper and acting crueller whenever I remembered what I was capable of when I'd used empathy in ways it shouldn't be used.

"Sully Sinclair," I said. "Hawk told me you're in the business of creating custom yachts?"

"Are you in the market?"

I glanced at Jethro who stayed to the side, allowing me to direct this conversation even though, up till now, I hadn't really considered making a high-end order for nautical equipment. Eleanor and I had discussed many ways to deliver unforgettable experiences for our troubled husbands and wives who stayed on Rapture, but I hadn't gone much further with the idea.

Ah well, I supposed now could work. The sooner I spoke to him, the sooner I could claim my wife from Nila Hawk and return to our quarters for privacy. "As a matter of fact, yes. I own a few islands in the Pacific, and my clients are used to a certain level of luxury." I smiled curtly. "Let's just say...I like to keep them happy."

In legal ways this time, instead of illegal.

"So you're after smaller vessels?"

"I'm after quite a few. Large and small. If you have time to discuss."

Eleanor should be here.

Rapture was her business venture, not mine. She'd been the one to turn a leased atoll into a highly profitable operation. I didn't want to step on her toes by ordering 'toys' as Jethro called them without her approval.

Jethro touched my shoulder. "I'll leave you gentlemen to discuss business. I'll come find you later, Sullivan."

I nodded as he vanished amongst a group of masked women. Once I made eye contact with Mr Prest, he sighed and held out his hand. "I can spare ten minutes."

Chapter Seven

THERE WERE MANY THINGS I loved in life.

Sully's gravelly voice in the morning as we rolled out of bed and into Nirvana, usually ending our early swim with a quickie before breakfast. Skittle's gentle feathers as she fluffed up in the crook of my shoulder. The juice of a lychee as I bit into the sweet fruit. The sunrises and sunsets that never failed to splash the horizon with every colour humans could name and many more that we couldn't.

I also loved the sounds of so many different animals. From the squeaks of otters, to the snuffles of pigs, and the click of fish grazing on coral beneath the sea.

But there was a special kind of love for the velveteen softness of a horse's nostrils.

Hot air cascaded over my fingers as the dapple grey huffed, scenting me and hopefully accepting me as a friend instead of foe. "She's gorgeous." I grinned, glancing at Nila as she undid her mask and dangled it from a fingertip.

"Her name is Warriors Don't Cry. Moth is her stable name." She drifted forward, grabbing a handful of oats from a large bin by the tack room. "She was a gift from my brother-in-law, Kestrel."

"That's an interesting name." I laughed as Moth gobbled up the oats from Nila's palm and blinked innocently for more. Her huge wise eyes framed in the thickest, blackest eyelashes.

"It's the family tradition of Hawk sons. A bird of prey is given as their nickname. Kes preferred his nickname to his real name." She threw me a grin. "I guess I can understand why."

"What was his real name?"

"Angus."

I wrinkled my nose. "Well, it's not going to win any sexy awards, but Gus is kind of cute."

Nila cocked her head. "Never thought about it that way. I always just thought of him as Kes. Our son is named in his honour."

I wanted to ask what happened, but the hushed way she spoke of him hinted he was no longer alive, and the tragedy still carried pain.

She strolled down the stables, laughing under her breath as a big black beast popped its head over the partition and whinnied. "Yes, Wings. I didn't forget about you."

I waited while she scooped up another handful of oats and fed the glistening ebony horse.

"He's stunning, too."

"He belongs to Jethro. Has a mind of his own and is steadfastly loyal to one person, but he tolerates treats from all of us." She scratched his forehead. "Don't you, grumpy pony?"

He snorted and disappeared back into his stall, biting his hay net with attitude.

Untying my own mask, I rubbed around my eyes and forehead where the material itched. "Do you ride every day?"

"We try to." Nila grinned, leading me back the way we'd come. Our heels clacked on the cobblestones as our dresses swished in the hay. "Our children were practically born in the saddle, so they have demands."

"From what I glimpsed of them, they seemed fearless."

Nila's eyes shadowed for a moment before she smiled. "I hope so. I hope they remain that way too."

We walked from the impressive stone stables, through the arched gateway, and back onto the pathway leading toward the bright lights and majesty of Hawksridge Hall. Guests had spilled out onto the deck leading from the ballroom; sounds of music and laughter winged over the lawns toward us. "You have a very lovely home."

She stopped and studied the hall as if she hadn't truly seen it in a while. Her head cocked to the side before shaking in disbelief. "You know? You're right. It *is* a home, isn't it?" She smiled brighter. "I think that's the first time it's been described as lovely before."

"What words are usually used?"

"Terrifying." She laughed. "Murderous. Deranged."

"Sully said there were rumours about your family and Jethro's." My eyes drifted to her diamond collar, reminding me that I had Hawk diamonds gracing my own body in the form of wedding rings. "That it involved debts and death."

"Yes, well." Her shoulders stiffened a little as she looked toward the huge pond twinkling with moonlight in the distance. She shivered as if a memory came and went. "Let's just say that there are things in the past we cannot change. But they had to happen to give us the future we now hold so precious."

A howl crested in the darkness, making me jump and look behind me. Did they have wolves on this damn estate?

"That's just Squirrel. Don't worry." Nila chuckled. "He's missing the freedom of running around with his pack. We kept them away from the hall tonight so the hounds didn't upset the guests."

"Hounds?"

"Yes, you know? Good for hunting and generally being a nuisance."

I flinched at the mention of hunting but kept my opinions about animal welfare to myself. "Are they friendly?"

Nila smirked as if she had an insider joke. "Friendly if you're not running for your life through the woods."

Something flashed in her dark eyes, making me pry when I probably shouldn't. "That sounds like there's a story there."

"Oh, there is." She moved closer, our dresses blending as we walked over manicured grass. "A very juicy story. One that involved me naked in a tree and Jethro chasing me on horseback."

"That does sound juicy."

She licked her lips. "Can...can I ask you a question?"

"Okay."

"Is it true that Sullivan created a drug that enables countless orgasms?"

I stiffened. "Where did you hear that?"

"Rumours have a tendency of trickling through all societies." She rubbed her lips. "Is it true?"

"Well, he's a pharmaceutical owner. He's created a great many things."

Nila nodded with a smirk. "How many orgasms does it give?"

My tension faded a little, sensing her curiosity and not judgment. I felt at ease with her as I did with Jess. Seemed even ladies in castles liked to talk about sex.

I quirked an eyebrow. "How many do you think you could handle in one night?"

She bit her lip, playfulness on her face. "Oh, I don't know. Six? Seven?"

"Try twenty. Thirty."

"Holy shit." She stopped walking. "You'd die."

"You're definitely catatonic afterward."

"Is it safe?"

"No." I gathered up a handful of my dress. "That's why he destroyed the vials he had left."

"Oh." Disappointment clouded her face. "Did it work on men?"

I flushed, thinking about Sully the morning I'd fed him elixir and the explosive sex we'd shared. The lust of it. The obsession of it. The danger of it. "Oh, yes. Yes, it *definitely* worked on men."

It worked so well, Sully almost died.

I almost died.

Jess almost died.

Elixir was poison hiding behind promises.

"Have you and your husband taken it?" Nila asked.

I nodded. I was sure the heated memories in my eyes gave her all the information she needed to know.

"I can imagine it was something."

"It was something alright." I stepped toward the glowing hall again.

"It's a shame it doesn't exist anymore. It would've been fun to have a night of debauchery. Jethro and I have a very active nightlife, but...I'd like to see just how wild he could become if he only had one thing to focus on and not hear so many things."

"Hear?"

"Oh." She waved her gloved hand. "Hear isn't the right word. He feels more than he hears. Senses, really. He's much, much better these days, but sometimes, I know he struggles. I'd like one night when he could just switch off and only have one desire. One thought. One need. It would be such a novel experience for him."

The way she said it made my heart squeeze. She loved her husband. She loved him as much as I loved Sully. It made me want to help, even if I didn't fully understand how. "Elixir was destroyed because it was far too potent, but...Sully made something in its place." I kept my voice low even though we were alone. "It's called *cinta*. Indonesian for love. It's nowhere near as dangerous, but it does amplify the lust already between you and your partner, and grants stamina to enjoy each other for longer than usual."

"What's it like?"

"It's like..." I paused, doing my best to describe it. "If a couple who had no lust for one another took it, they might get a small burn to be together. But if a couple already wants each other—if there is that undeniable crackle of chemistry that links your blood to his...it's incredible. It takes your natural lust and amplifies it. It becomes *everything*. Every touch is foreplay. Every kiss is...well—" I blushed. "Let's just say, if you want your husband as much as I want mine, a kiss can be orgasmic. Unlike elixir, *cinta* doesn't overload your system with fake desire but magnifies your own to the point where it's impossible to ignore."

I smiled, remembering the first time Sully had given us a dose on our wedding night. Still healing from broken bones and muscles weak from his coma, *cinta* had ensured we'd consummated our marriage *extremely* thoroughly.

We didn't use it every time we had sex—Sully was walking elixir to me without needing other stimulants—but on those nights when it was just us, and we fancied stepping into a world of myth with a VR fantasy—where any place and any time could be experienced—we'd dabble.

We'd share a drop of *cinta* and lose ourselves to nothing but love and lust.

I thought about what I'd packed in our suitcase. What I'd brought, just in case Sully and I needed a break from England before we were able to go home.

"Wow, sounds great." Nila smiled. "Ah well, if your husband ever decides to sell his magic, I'd like to see if I can give Jethro a night where the rest of the world falls away and it's just us." Arching her chin at the hall, she added, "Come on, we better go back. The men will be wondering."

I followed her, my mind racing. Whatever drugs Sully had cooked up for Jethro's condition when he was younger were now obsolete thanks to Nila's love and presence. But...if we could give them a night where there were no other thoughts, responsibilities, or interruptions caused by whatever Jethro suffered, then...I wanted to give them that.

Before we left Hawksridge Hall, I would give Nila a gift.

A small box with the keys to a whole other world.

A world accessed only by virtual reality, desire, and togetherness.

Sullivan

Chapter Eight

"FOUND YOU." I WRAPPED my arms around Eleanor as she brushed past, her fingers hastily tying her mask back into place. Nuzzling against her neck, I inhaled her, groaning at the scent of orchids, her, and the crispness of English air. "I missed you."

I'd finished with Mr Prest.

I'd garnered all I needed to know about him, even with his face obscured by a mask. Despite the ruthlessness surrounding him, he seemed legit in his yacht endeavours, and the quick photos he'd shown me on his phone indicated an exemplary product. He'd promised to send through a quote with a range of vessels so I could go over it with Eleanor and see if it was a worthy addition to Rapture and its guests.

As far as I was concerned, I'd been friendly with Jethro. I'd been polite with Mr Prest. I'd put in an appearance and socialised for long enough.

Now, I wanted to be alone.

With my delicious fucking wife.

She shivered as I pressed a kiss against her throat. "I missed you too."

"I'll see you later, Eleanor." Nila waved, vanishing into the ballroom in search of her husband.

Eleanor raised her hand weakly in goodbye, her body melting

in my arms as I licked the shell of her ear. "I'm about done with this shindig. You?" I sucked her sunburst diamond earring into my mouth. "I've had a hard-on since our dance. I can't stop thinking about being inside you." Dropping my hand down her belly, I pressed her ass against me. "Feel that, Jinx? That's your fucking fault, and I'm done waiting."

Her head tipped back, landing on my chest. Her long hair wedged against us. "Found a closet we can disappear into?"

"A closet won't do." I arched my hips into her ass, grateful no one else was in the shadowy corridor. "I want all of you. I want you naked and begging. I want to take my time and ensure you're as desperate as I am."

"Oh, I'm pretty sure I'm as desperate as you." She laughed softly, her breath catching as I fisted her breast, squeezing her nipple through the iridescent material of her ball gown. "Sully..."

"Let's go." Releasing her, I grabbed her hand and dragged her away from the masquerade.

"Wait. Do we need to say goodnight? Is it rude if we—"

"It's rude if I spend the entire night with an obvious erection."

She smiled, her gaze dropping down my front. "I could get on my knees and help you with that."

I grinned savagely. "Oh, you'll be on your knees alright. But then I intend to repay the favour with my head between your thighs."

Her eyes hooded. "How is that you can make me wet in two seconds flat?"

"How is that you can make me so fucking hard when I had you only a few hours ago?"

"It's a curse."

I cupped my hand around her nape, jerking her into me. Our lips touched as I fed words into her mouth. "The best kind of curse."

I kissed her.

Hard.

Our noses brushed, our masks clacked, and our tongues broke free at the same time, dancing, licking, desperate to drop all pretences of being human and give in to the animals within us.

Struggling to catch a proper breath, I stumbled back and dragged my gorgeous wife down the corridor, past suits of armour, tapestries, masterpieces, and weaponry. We stopped halfway up the staircase, desperation ensuring another fierce and furious kiss before we practically ran the rest of the way to our room.

Wrenching open the door, I tossed her inside before locking it and ripping off my tuxedo blazer.

If I didn't get out of these clothes soon, I'd tear them off, and I didn't want to show such disrespect to Nila's sewing wizardry.

Eleanor backed up, her grey gaze hot and hungry on mine. She licked her lips as I forced myself to be gentle and undo the buttons of my silver shirt instead of ripping them to shreds.

"I suggest you remove that dress, Jinx. Otherwise, you'll have a lot of apologies to make in the morning when Nila requests her gown back and finds it in pieces."

She swallowed hard, backing toward the suitcase by one of the huge full-length windows. Staff had entered while we were at the masquerade and drawn the crimson velvet drapes, ensuring no one from outside could see what we were about to indulge in.

"I...I have something." She kept moving away from me as I kicked off my shoes and wrenched off my socks.

"Whatever it is doesn't matter. Strip, Eleanor. I won't fucking ask again."

She dashed to the suitcase, tore off her long gloves, and unzipped the top pocket. Pulling something out, she copied me and kicked off her high heels, before padding toward the huge mattress and four-poster bed.

Placing the box on the coverlets, she stood in front of it so I couldn't see all while she undid her mask, shook out her hair, and reached behind her to undo the laces of her gown.

She wasn't fast enough.

Marching toward her, I spun her around. "Let me."

She gasped as I worked on the fastenings, pulling on the ribbon trapping her inside. Her chest rose and fell as I loosened the tight material, spilling her breasts free and making my cock weep to be inside her. "Christ, you're stunning."

I cupped her breasts, kneading her with paws that couldn't be gentle.

She turned to face me as the dress puddled to the floor, leaving her in just a pair of sheer knickers. She hadn't bothered to wear stockings—not willing to wear uncomfortable clothing after living five years basically nude in the tropics.

Her stomach fluttered with eager breath and her hands shook as they reached for my belt, undoing the buckle, then unzipping my fly.

Locking eyes with me, she inserted her hand into my boxer-briefs and fisted my erection.

"*Fuck.*" My head fell back as she pumped me. No teasing, just torment.

In a rustle of lace, she dropped to her knees.

I swallowed back a growl as her lips wrapped around my cock, her tongue instantly licking at the slit, making me fucking insane.

My hands slipped through her hair, holding the silky chocolate strands, allowing her to suck me but also reminding her who was in charge.

Her head bobbed, her hand dropping to cup my balls while she sucked and ensured I was ready to come in two fucking seconds. The temptation to explode down her throat almost undid me. The way she knew exactly how to make me lose it. The power she had over me made me aggressive with the desire to use her.

My mind swam as lust became even headier.

She whimpered around my girth, making my ass clench to drive into her and a ripple of precum threaten that I was moments away from splintering apart. My vision turned hazy as I looked down at her on her knees before me.

A tsunami of love hit me.

I drowned beneath how much I fucking adored her, worshipped her, and wanted to destroy her all at once. Her saliva glistened around my cock where it disappeared into her mouth. Her teeth teased my skin as I arched into her, feeding more length onto her tongue, and her eyes spoke the same message that mine did.

She loved me back.

Fuck, I'm so goddamn lucky.

I rolled forward, my balance faltering.

My gaze locked on the bed behind her where she'd put the box.

I froze.

Lust magnified until my voice echoed with feral desire. "You brought the sensors."

Eleanor nodded, her mouth still locked around my cock. Slowly, she pulled away and licked her lips. "I bought *cinta* too. Not that we need it." She squirmed on the floor. "If you don't touch me soon, I'm going to come just from sucking you."

Dropping my hands from her hair, I cupped under her elbows and hoisted her from the carpet. Throwing her backward onto the bed, I made sure she didn't land on the box, and the moment she bounced on her back and her legs splayed, I pounced.

The bed was so high, it was a convenient level to bend at the waist and press my mouth against her pussy. I ripped her underwear down her legs, leaving her bare.

Her spine arched off the mattress. Her fingernails scratched my scalp. And she wasn't kidding with how needy she was.

She came the moment I thrust my tongue inside her.

"Oh, *God*." Her inner muscles throbbed around my invasion. Her clit swelled in my mouth. Her taste consumed me, and I grew fucking drunk on her pleasure.

I licked and bit all while she broke apart, dragging out her orgasm until she thrashed and tried to push my head away. "Sensitive."

I kept licking, inserting two fingers inside her, loving how wet she was.

"Sully!" Her hand latched on my wrist, preventing me from driving back inside her. "That felt too good."

Obeying her need to recover, I stood and wiped at her wetness smeared on my chin. "Better?"

"Just getting started." She lay naked with her legs spread, her eyes no longer grey but silver with sexual need. "Come here. I want you inside me."

I clucked my tongue. "Patience, my dear Jinx." Grabbing the box, I opened it to find she'd brought four lots of sensors and a bottle of *cinta*. I shuddered at the thought of dabbling in the drug tonight.

We were both worked up.

If we took it, there'd be no stopping us. We'd be at it all fucking night.

Sounds like a fabulous idea.

What Jethro didn't know wouldn't hurt him. He didn't need to know if Eleanor and I christened every inch of this suite while deep in the VR world of a fantasy.

Eleanor never took her eyes off me as I pulled out the eye lenses and earbuds. "Sit up."

She obeyed instantly, allowing me to place the lenses over her stunning pupils and gently insert the earbuds.

She blinked, encouraging her vision to accept the obstruction. While she acclimatised, I placed the second lot of lenses over my own eyes and inserted two earbuds. We'd long since stopped using the other sensors. Why did we need to obstruct touch and taste when we already lived a fantasy?

Bending, I removed my trousers and pulled my cell phone free from the pocket.

Eleanor sucked in a breath as I pulled up the app for Euphoria and the many cyphered fantasies that we'd enjoyed, yet to enjoy, and a few I hadn't finished coding.

"What do you want?" I asked, my voice still rough and dark. "A dungeon like we joked about? A picnic where everyone watches me eat you for lunch? How about a dark alley where you beg me not to fuck you?"

Eleanor deliberately ran a finger over her bottom lip, ratcheting up my lust until my heart pounded in my chest. "What do *you* want?" She blinked as if an idea sprang to mind. "What's your deepest, darkest fantasy, Sully Sinclair?" She scooted onto her knees, and her breasts jiggled as she added, "Take me there. Do whatever you want to me."

I cocked my head. "My fantasy? What about yours?"

"We can do mine another time." She raked her eyes down my nakedness, fixating on my throbbing cock. "I want to know yours."

My thumb scrolled absently through the many lines of codes. Fantasies that guests had requested. Others that I'd made just for backup. And one that I'd done my best to forget.

Clicking on the bottom link, I mulled over what this could do.

I did have one experience I hadn't shared or sold.

I'd programmed a particular hallucination only a few days after buying Jinx. The fantasy had popped into my head while I'd tossed and turned, unable to sleep, burning up with fucking want for her.

Instead of giving in and going to her villa, I'd typed the code and come from the illusion. Buying myself more time before I admitted to myself how helplessly fucked I was when it came to her.

It wasn't the typical dominant fantasy, sharing, or even voyeuristic.

It was…weird really.

Singularly mine and odd in so many ways.

Which all fantasies were, really.

I'd learned that truth with the peculiar perversions of my guests over the years.

Eleanor watched me carefully, understanding sparking in her gaze. "You already have one, don't you?"

"It's not what you think," I growled. "It's not even a fantasy per sey, more of a playground where I'm most free."

"Sounds perfect. Let's go." Eleanor smiled, holding out her hand for me to place mine in hers. "Press the button, Sully."

I bit my bottom lip, glancing around the suite. As long as we stayed here, we would have privacy. However, if our inhibitions became too consumed by the illusion, who the hell knew where we'd end up.

Jethro and his wife might find us fucking on his lawn if we weren't careful, completely unhinged and in a totally different world to this one.

Precautions are needed.

Locking my phone screen, I clutched it in my fist as I marched naked to the bathroom where two fluffy bathrobes hung on diamante hooks.

Ripping out the belts, I carried both back to Eleanor who'd scooted onto her knees to track me. "Stand up," I commanded, smirking when she launched herself to the rich carpeted floor, anticipation and need glowing on her skin.

"Eager, Eleanor?" I murmured as I ducked to my haunches and tied her ankle to the bedframe.

"You have no idea." She shuddered as I ran my fingers up the back of her leg, stroking the sensitive skin behind her knee before creeping up, up, up, and running a gentle touch through the hot slipperiness of her pussy.

"Oh, I think I do." I inserted the tip of my finger, falling head over heels in love with her all over again as she grabbed my wrist and forced my touch higher inside her. "Fuck, you're going to pay for that."

She groaned, her gaze dilated and fixated on my nakedness. Her hips rocked on my hand. "I'll happily pay whatever you want if you put me out of my misery."

"Anything?" I slid my arm around her waist, jerking her against me. I inserted another finger, stretching her, making her writhe in my arms. "Would you let me tie you up? Have you in any position? Do whatever I fucking wanted?"

"God, yes."

My thumb rubbed her clit, her inner muscles clenching around my fingers. "You're mine. Do you deny it?"

She struggled to raise her hand, flashing her wedding and engagement rings in my face. "Legally yours and wholeheartedly."

My cock throbbed, leaking another droplet of demented desire. "You say the sweetest things."

"I try." She snapped her teeth. "But I won't stay sweet unless you deliver what you're promising."

"Patience, filthy Jinx." Removing my hand from her pussy, I bent and tied my own ankle, her wetness on my fingers making the knot slippery. At least this way, we would stay behind closed doors.

Pushing her away a little, I leaned over the bed and grabbed the bottle of *cinta*. I shook it, raising my eyebrow. "You're drenched already. I'm hard as a fucking rock. We both don't need this, but...fancy turning our sexual hunger into a famine?"

She licked her lips, her cheeks flushed. "Adding fuel to the fire?"

"Pouring an entire drum of gasoline."

Her chest rose and fell. "I can't promise I'll be able to control it. I'm already out of my mind with lust."

"Guess we'll find out how wild we can be." I kissed her, pressing my skin to hers and adding another layer of electrical heat.

Bad idea.

Her mouth opened wide.

Her tongue lashed over mine.

A simple kiss exploded into a teeth-clacking, dry-humping inferno. It would be so easy to hoist her up my body and plunge inside her. So fucking tempting to thrust—

Tearing my mouth away, I snarled, "Open."

Panting, she did as she was told, blinking rapidly while swaying on her feet.

Squeezing the dropper, I unscrewed the bottle and hovered the glass dispenser over her tongue. She never looked away as I squeezed one droplet into her mouth.

Her eyes closed as she swallowed, making my stomach clench and cock bob with desire. Tipping my head back, I swallowed my own dose before fastening the bottle and tossing it back onto the bed.

The recipe in this particular drug was a much safer, saner version of elixir. It didn't hijack neural pathways or take over mental capacity and blood flow. There was no risk of a heart attack like its predecessor.

Cinta merely took what lust was already there and increased it to a level where the host felt drunk. Where any and all self-consciousness was deleted, and the only thought in your entire body was to be connected with your significant other.

That was why it worked so well for our unhappily married couples who came for counselling. Strip back the arguments, the grudges, and the past, and you were left with a healthy fresh start centred entirely on basic chemistry.

Eleanor moaned under her breath as she reached for me. Her nipples peaked, and a trickle of need slid down her inner thigh. Her fingers hissed with power, shocking my skin as she stepped into me.

My balls tightened. My pulse hitched.

I wanted her so fucking much.

But not here.

Tonight, we'd attended a ball in costumes and disguises.

Now…we were free to visit a place far more fitting.

We were free to be *us*.

Unlocking my phone, I highlighted the link I'd never loaded before and pressed the button.

Chapter Nine

I BLINKED AS AN entirely new world unfolded before me.

The chirps of birds pierced my comprehension first. The babble of a brook. The crash of a waterfall. The exotic hum of cicadas in the trees serenading with a tropical symphony.

Unlike previous fantasies that loaded in complete detail, this one evolved from white nothingness into the most extraordinary jungle. Palm trees soared from soil. Leaf matter littered the earth. Glossy bushes, vibrant flowers, and sweeping banyan trees all swept toward the skies.

Once the trees were in place, vines dripped from their branches, delivering bromeliads and jewelled frogs and the intricate ecosystem of a humid forest.

The bird and cicada song was drowned out as monkeys chattered in the treetops, and the snuffle of wild pigs and slither of snakes whispered in the undergrowth.

Everywhere I looked, life existed.

Not just flora but fauna too.

A deer bounded off in a spiel of sunlight.

A black panther slinked up a tree trunk.

A toucan flew low with its beak glistening with colour.

And then, there was Sully.

A man with two legs and two arms but the heart of a beast

who belonged wholeheartedly in a place of wilderness over any castle or city.

I swallowed a gasp as I drank him in.

His hair was slightly longer, teasing the tops of his shoulders, loose and tangled. His delicious body was bare apart from a simple loincloth made of softened, plaited reeds. His sun-browned stomach rippled with ridges and power. His arms bunched as he fisted his hands by muscular thighs. His feet planted into the soft dirt, and his head cocked like a predator just sensing which way his prey would run.

He hadn't changed his outward appearance. He still looked like my husband in every delicious way possible. Just…untamed.

He grinned as his gaze dropped from mine and skated down my body. "Hello, darling wife. I see my choice of wardrobe suits you well."

I followed his stare, fingering the strung shells and delicate beads on multiple cords around my neck. They hung low, dipping into my cleavage with a jingle and jangle of jewels.

My hair was loose and tickled my naked back. My breasts were bare, my ankles were decorated with strings of more beads and shells, and on my hips hung a simple flaxen skirt.

I looked as primitive as him.

As wild as him.

I grinned. "Is this what you fantasise about when I'm wearing actual clothes?"

"It's what I jerk off to when you're not around."

I stepped toward him, letting a spike of jealousy taint my tone. "You pleasure yourself without waiting for me?"

He matched my step, closing the distance between us. "I have no choice. You've bewitched me, woman. I can't expect you to serve me every time I have a dirty thought about you."

"You can." I reached out to touch the turquoise macaw feather that fluttered from the treetops and snagged in Sully's hair. "I want you to."

He shuddered as my fingertips grazed his cheek. "I want you now."

"How much?"

Grabbing my wrist, he fanned my fingers and pressed them under his loincloth. "So fucking much."

I fisted his cock.

He grunted and swayed, his eyes shooting shards of temper. His loincloth didn't wrap between his legs, leaving the heavy weight of his balls and the thickened steel of his erection bare.

I took full advantage.

Stroking him, I murmured, "It feels like you want me a lot."

He bit his lip, turning him from sexy to downright fuckable. "I'm barely holding on."

"Then let go." I wedged my thumb against the top of his cock, pressing down and making him jolt. "I *want* you to let go."

Sucking in a breath, he wrapped his hand around my nape and jerked me into him. His lips met my ear, and his hot command slipped directly into my soul. "What I want is for you to run, gorgeous Eleanor."

A second passed.

My heart pounded.

He pulled away, and our eyes locked.

His eyebrow cocked as he looked over my shoulder to the wild forest behind me. I'd run from him when he'd been high on elixir, and that had ended with us fornicating until he almost drowned.

That part had been terrifying, but the rest? The chase, the hunt, the pounce, the mount...it'd been dangerously erotic.

Dropping his hand from my nape and removing my fingers from his cock, he breathed, "*Run.*"

Fire shot down my legs.

Lust exploded into every extremity.

I ran.

I spun and bolted, leaping over fallen logs and vanishing into the thicket of vines, humidity, and undergrowth. My necklaces tinkled a runaway song. My anklets tickled my legs. My flaxen skirt kissed my naked thighs. And every element added to the snarling thirst in my blood for him. For Sully. For sex.

I ran even though I wanted him to catch me.

Wetness slid down my inner thigh as my brain flickered between self-preservation and sacrificing myself to his sexual fury.

Sully didn't chase initially.

His snarl-filled groan was the only thing that followed as I galloped through the thick foliage.

But then the crash of his attack sounded, the thud of heavy footfalls coming after me.

My heart flurried in panic, swamping with demented need. *Cinta*-amplified lust fogged my thoughts until my vision hazed with it. Until I gasped and mewled for it.

I needed him.

So fucking much.

I wanted to fall to my knees and let him trap me.

I wanted him to beg to claim me.

I wanted to beg.

I wanted us linked and writhing, thrusting and coming.

I couldn't explain the raw desire that fleeing from him gave me. The primordial triggers of being mounted and claimed, blending with the undeniable hunger to be used. As graphically and as brutally as possible.

No matter how many fancy clothes or intricate words we spoke as a species, we were still just beasts at heart.

Beasts who wanted to maul and—

"When I catch you, Jinx, I want to hear you scream as I fuck you."

Oh, God.

My breath caught as I dodged around a palm tree, running deeper into whatever illusion Sully had programmed. Unlike the pine forest where Drake had met his end, this one never stopped. There was no portal to return me back to the centre of the illusion. The pathways and animal tracks kept guiding me farther into density.

Breathing hard, I ran swifter.

I exploded from the thick undergrowth beside a river's edge. Ferns bobbed in the muggy breeze. Parrots darted in the sun. Dragonflies hovered and lizards sun-baked and fish glittered in the stream.

So much beauty.

So much peace.

Arms lashed around me from behind.

Sully's harsh breath filled my ear as he kicked apart my ankles and lowered me to the ground in one swift move. "Caught you." His teeth scraped the back of my neck as he collapsed to his knees behind me. "Fuck, you're gorgeous."

My necklaces jangled as he fisted my breasts. Pinching my nipples, he groaned as his hips thrust against me. "Christ, I can't control myself around you. I've never been able to."

Dropping his touch, he found my flaxen skirt and tore it to sinful shreds. One moment, it hid my decency, and the next, it was in tatters by my knees.

I moaned as his fingers bit into my hip bones, pulling me back into him. "Every day, I thank fucking fate for delivering you. Every night, I dream of losing you. Every moment, I can't believe you're mine."

Bowing over me, he nudged his cock against my wetness. "Mine to adore, to cherish, to *fuck*."

I bit my lip, waiting for him to thrust inside.

But he waited.

One heartbeat, two, three.

"You're all mine, Eleanor. My perfect lovely wife." His heart pounded on my spine and his body radiated erotic heat. "I will never take a second with you for granted." Running his cock up and down my pussy, he growled long and low. "So wet. So ready. Do you want me, Jinx?"

My head bobbed. My breath came too quick. "Yes. God, yes. Please—"

He drove upward, inward, deep, deep, *deep*. "Take me. Take all of fucking me."

I screamed.

Just like he promised.

His cock stretched me in so many familiar and dominating ways. My fingers scratched at the earth, my elbows threatened to buckle, and my breasts swung as he pounded inside me, furious and fierce.

My necklaces jingled as he struck a punishing, brutalising rhythm.

We'd made love before.

We'd kissed with sultry passion and rocked in dirty pleasure. But this?

This was pure, uninhibited fucking.

"Christ." Sully's roar bounced off the river and ricocheted in the trees. His pace as he rutted into me struck the fuse on my *cinta*-amplified desire and triggered an orgasm that detonated with crucifying pressure.

It bolted up my legs, fissured around my womb, and supernovaed outward in thick, pulsing waves of exquisite pleasure.

He followed me, spurting inside me, marking me as his. His head fell back, his fingers dug into my hips, and he jerked with agonising bliss.

When our climaxes allowed the virtual reality world to return and our hearts to find a healthier rhythm, Sully chuckled under his breath. "You'll be the death of me one day, Eleanor. Each time I think I can't come any harder, I'm proven wrong." Hugging me from behind, he played with the pretty necklaces dangling off my neck.

"My very own Amazonian princess. Ripe and ready for my taking."

I wriggled my hips where we were still linked. Him inside me. His body within mine. The very epitome of male, female connection. "If I'm a princess, why am I on my knees in the dirt?"

He nuzzled the back of my neck. "Because you're also a goddess of debauchery and are better suited to such places, especially when my cock is deep inside you." He rolled his hips for good measure.

Thanks to *cinta,* he would stay hard for however long our lust remained. Our neurological system wasn't hijacked like with elixir. We had control of this mania.

If we let our systems be sated from this session, our playtime could be over. Or…if we wanted to stay aroused for another and another…and another, then our bodies would very willingly oblige.

I hadn't had my fill.

And Sully's voice smoked with sex, hinting he planned on corrupting me for many more hours to come.

Luckily, we were in a giant mansion where other guests wouldn't hear our cries of rapture. If they did, they'd think our greedy moans were the echoes of haunting ghosts.

With a quick kiss to my sweaty shoulder blades, Sully withdrew and stood. Bending, he collected me from the river's edge and spun me into his arms.

We stood like that for a minute.

Just being.

Gathered in a hug that allowed our hearts to connect as violently as our bodies had.

Winding my arms around his waist, I pressed my cheek to his chest, feeling the rightness of my world. The sense of belonging and soul-deep contentment of our unshakeable bond.

Slowly, Sully kissed the top of my head and pushed me away a little. "Well, as far as appetisers go, that wasn't bad."

I grinned. "That was the hors d'oeuvres, huh? What's for the main meal?"

His eyes flashed with cunning sex appeal. "Oh, I have an idea."

"You do, do you?"

"I definitely do." Taking my hand, he tugged me into the jungle. "Come along. I'll show you."

Sullivan

Chapter Ten

"YOU PROGRAMMED THIS?"

Eleanor gawked at the treehouse as she climbed the final rung up the rope ladder and stepped foot into the bamboo creation.

The skin around her hips was bruised from my fingers. Her nipples still pebbled. Her lips red from my kisses. Naked, apart from the anklets and necklaces, with leaves and flower petals twined in her hair, she looked every bit a figment of this fantasy as the cyphered palms, wildlife, and sunshine.

Thank God, she wasn't.

Thank everything holy that she was *real*. Because if she wasn't...I would never want to live in the real world again. I would live here, in this VR perfection, where I could keep her forever.

Running her fingers along the carved banister and entering the two-story treehouse, she whistled under her breath. "I have no idea how much coding is needed for these fantasies, but this is impressive, Sully."

I followed her, equally as undressed and not caring that my cock hung heavy with want, hidden by a piece of braided flax. "It's easy once you know what you're doing."

"Have you visited this place before?" She eyed up the mattress beneath a mosquito net, similar to the one we had at home in Indonesia. The bedroom was simple with bamboo slatted walls, huge open-air windows with no glass, exposed rafters, and a roof made of palm leaves.

A sitting area carved from banyan wood and teak waited by the bed, angled to see the stars through the canopy. Simple, uncluttered, and natural. I could live here permanently.

"No. I've never visited," I said, catching her gaze as she looked above to the single ladder leading to the mezzanine level above.

"How do you know if you've got the code right? What happens if you'd programmed a floor that was paper-thin or trees that were poisonous?"

I shrugged. "Codes are simple. They're just ones and zeros. As long as you follow basic parameters, not much can go wrong."

"Yet you create myth out of reality." She grinned, her hair loose and tangled and oh, so fucking tempting. "I'm impressed."

I smiled, slow and sultry. "*How* impressed?"

Her grin switched to a smirk of invitation. "Very. I can show you…if you want?"

"I'm going to take you up on that offer. Soon." I stalked toward her, crowding her toward the ladder leading up to the next level. "But for now, up."

She blinked, looking over her shoulder. "Up there?"

I nodded.

"What's up there?" she asked, her voice low and hypnotising.

My cock jerked under my loincloth, and I struggled not to take her right here, right now. I could. There was no reason I should wait. But I had a surprise, and I wanted to deliver it before I had her again.

"You'll see." I put my hands on her delicate shoulders and spun her to face the ladder. Smacking her bare ass, I commanded, "Climb."

She muttered something under her breath. Something belligerent that fired my lust and had me crowding her against the ladder.

She gasped as I dropped my hand between her legs and fingered her from behind. "Care to repeat what you just said?"

She moaned as I slipped one finger inside. Wet and hot and greedy.

Biting her bottom lip, she shook her head, her eyes closed and forehead furrowed with need.

I inserted another finger, stretching her. Ensuring my cock bobbed and the hunger to thrust inside her amplified. "Tell me and I might let you come."

Air exploded from her lungs as I drove up, catching her clit. Her legs buckled. I caught her, holding her at my mercy.

"I said you're so bossy."

"And the other part..."

"If you heard me, why do I have to repeat it?"

I withdrew only to drive my fingers upward again, making her pant and squirm. "Because you ought to know such things come with consequences."

"What consequences?" She gasped as I fingered her faster, driving her into madness.

"So many fucking consequences." I kissed her throat, unsheathing my teeth to bite right over her artery. My teeth tingled to puncture her skin. My instincts more primitive than restrained at that moment. "Repeat what you said, Jinx. And I might show you my surprise."

Her hips rocked backward, bumping into my throbbing erection. "Your surprise being your cock?"

I bit her harder, rubbing myself against the seam of her ass. "I'll give you my cock in a way you haven't experienced before."

She shivered. "Show me."

"Do what I commanded first." I pulled my fingers free, spreading her wet desire over her belly as I stroked my way to her heavy breasts. Her necklaces clinked as I shoved them aside and pinched her nipples. "Do it."

She groaned as I touched her, wobbling in my hold. "I said you're bossy and controlling...and still act as if you own me when really...I own *you*."

"Did you pay half a million dollars for me?" I kissed along her throat, inhaling her wicked scent of orchids and whatever perfumed body wash the Hawks stocked in their showers.

"No. And besides, I now own every penny you have, so technically that money is mine and I am priceless."

"That might be, but did you kidnap and hold me hostage?"

"Yes. Hell, yes," she moaned as I squeezed her breasts. One in each hand, claiming her for my own. "You might've paid money to steal me, Sully, but the moment we met, it was me who stole you."

"And you think that gives you power over me?" I rocked my hips into her, faster and harder, driving myself to an orgasm just from pure friction.

"Definitely." She gasped as I kicked her legs apart. Screw the surprise. She needed reminding who was in charge.

Who owned who?

I did.

I owned every part of her because I couldn't survive if I didn't.

It didn't matter that every word she moaned was right.

She owned me.

She'd corrupted me the second she'd landed on my shores.

"You might regret saying that, Jinx." I grabbed the base of my cock and shoved away the loincloth, lining up with her pussy. "I might need to give you a lesson in ownership."

"And prove my point?" She looked over her shoulder at me. "That you belong to me? That I can make you kneel with just a word or beg at my feet with just a touch?"

"The point being you own a monster, not just a man in love with you." I thrust.

Swift and savage.

I stabbed inside her with no finesse, and her mouth opened on a silent scream. Cupping her throat, I tilted her head back until my lips slammed over hers, swallowing that silent scream, kissing her as deep as I could.

She convulsed in my arms as I drove up into her again and again. I fucked her against the ladder, dropping all my guards and defences.

Her hands clawed at the rungs, doing her best to withstand my takeover, all while her legs spread in wanton welcome.

"Yes. Oh, *god,* yes," she hissed, her mouth slick and hot beneath mine.

Our tongues tangled and knotted as we gave ourselves over to basic copulation. We didn't touch other than where our bodies connected. My hands planted over hers on the rungs, giving me purchase to thrust harder and fiercer inside her.

I wanted her to have bruises.

I wanted her to feel my possession for days after this.

"I own your every breath, Eleanor. Do you deny it?" I kissed her faster, messier. "I own your moans, your begs, your vows. Try to say that I don't."

She shook her head, her mouth seeking mine, a bone-deep gasp shaking her as I continued to pump hard. "I don't. I don't deny it." Her cheeks flushed, and her eyes snapped closed as I let go of every humanity and gave everything that I was to this woman.

I fed her my body and my heart.

I let her feel my trembles at how honoured I was to fuck her.

I let her see my soul at how privileged I was to love her.

And when she let go, matching me in every broken way possible, I came.

I jerked and spurted into my gorgeous wife and cried out as her own release followed mine; her inner muscles milking my cock, the powerful waves of pleasure dragging out the final lapse of my own.

As quickly as our lovemaking began, it was over, and we both stood there, breathing hard with our shared climaxes sticky and binding us together.

Nudging away her heat-damp hair, I kissed her nape. "I will never get enough of you."

"I'm glad." She groaned as I withdrew, wincing a little at the sensitivity. "Ditto."

A droplet of our combined orgasms plopped to the bamboo floor.

Eleanor blushed. "Good job this is a fantasy. Otherwise, I'd be mopping these floors later."

I grinned. "I'm sure a maid fantasy could be arranged. Now that you've mentioned it, I could happily indulge in a rich aristocrat having his horny way with the innocent housekeeper."

"Write it." She turned to kiss me, standing on her cute tiptoes. "I'd like to try that one."

"Consider it done." I smiled, gently kissing her back before spinning her to face the ladder. "Now, get your sexy ass up there. I have a surprise for you."

Chapter Eleven

CLIMBING UP THE LADDER, I had no idea what to expect on the second level.

Another bedroom perhaps? Maybe a small sitting area?

"It's...empty." I turned to face Sully as he climbed up behind me, his overbearing presence and power making the space feel tight and constricted.

Giving me a half-smile, he marched to the small door at the back. "We're not there yet." Sweeping it open, he revealed yet another platform. This one outdoors, canopied by hanging trees, vines, and utterly at one with the jungle.

"Oh, wow." I stepped from indoors to outdoors, marvelling at the attention to detail Sully went with the VR creation. Heavy flowers in mauves and maroons hung over the balustrade. Bamboo carved lanterns dotted all four corners of the deck and sunlight spangled through the leaves and trunks to stencil the flooring with a golden glow.

There was no furniture, no clutter. Just the backdrop of nature in all its beauty.

Sully sighed as he joined me, drinking in perfection, smiling at a flock of parrots as they darted past.

The flash of jewelled feathers made me miss Pika and Skittles. Even though our minds were currently in the tropics of some fictional forest, our bodies were in England. If I focused on reality instead of myth, I felt the chill of English weather and the mustiness of an ancient hall.

Goddess Isles was never cold, never damp, never musty. It was forever tropical and temperate, and I found it surprising how homesick I was, considering we'd only been gone a single day.

A crash sounded in the canopy, making me spin around, my necklaces clinking on my chest. A beautifully patterned feline slinked from the branches, leaping gracefully onto the deck with its tail flicking and amber eyes narrowed with intelligence.

I froze.

Fantasy or not, I didn't fancy pissing off a jaguar. "Eh, Sully?" I didn't move, relying on him to resolve this uncomfortable situation.

I was naked.

Sully still wore his loincloth.

And the cat had claws sharp enough to disembowel us with one swipe.

"It won't hurt you, Eleanor." Sully stepped forward, a soft smile on his face. "Will you, jaguar?"

The cat sat on its haunches and yawned, revealing the longest canines I'd ever seen. Its tongue curled and stuck out in a pink lash as it snarled on the tail of its yawn.

Its pelt was velvet and pigmented with circlets of brown, tan, and cream, mottling its presence to move unseen in the foliage. The natural camouflage was a work of art, even if it was a highly equipped predator who obeyed no one but its own desires.

Goosebumps spread over me.

I wrapped arms around my nakedness and backed up a step. "You programmed everything? Even that?"

Sully looked at me before padding toward the giant jungle beast. "The codes for the animals I copied from the cypher that Drake locked you in."

I frowned, struggling to remember if I'd seen that particular jaguar in the campsite when I'd been dressed as a native and Drake had been some raping lumberjack who thought he could take what he wasn't allowed. "The animals only arrived later. After..." I swallowed, remembering in full detail how the fantasy had switched from daylight to darkness and wolves the sizes of cars had magically appeared. "After you entered the illusion." I shivered, recalling how Sully had come for me. How he'd fought against all odds, ignored broken bones and rapidly fading heartbeats, and conjured a monster with scaled flesh, venomous fangs, and devil horns.

He'd saved me by putting me to sleep. He'd freed me of the fantasy, and I'd never know what he did to Drake, deep within a hallucination that was never about pleasure just revenge.

Keeping my eyes on the jaguar, I murmured, "I never asked you what happened that day, but now, I'm curious." I braced myself, waiting until Sully made eye contact with me. His blazing blue stare shielded with secrets. "How did you break Drake's mind?"

Sully froze, his stomach rippling with muscle. "Do you seriously want to know?" Shaking away his stillness, he closed the distance to the jaguar that sat watching us like we were fish caught in a bowl. Holding out his hand, he showed no fear as he stroked the big cat's velvety head.

I swallowed a gasp as the cat instantly purred and bumped against Sully to be petted harder. The sight of a wild man stroking a hunter, high up in the treetops, dressed in just a loincloth, scrambled my grasp on what was real and what was his illusion.

Sully *belonged* here.

He belonged in an untouched utopia where he wore sunlight instead of suits and had all the gifts of survival for a raw, undomesticated existence instead of a billionaire pharmaceutical empire.

Funny, how he had everything that people fought and clawed to earn. He'd mastered the corporate world. He'd dabbled in the unethical and illegal. He'd turned his back on nefarious enterprises and given me everything he was the day he married me…yet, Sully Sinclair didn't need, nor want any of those things.

He just wanted to be left alone.

To be free in the wild with creatures and elements.

And me.

The truth punched me in the heart and made me love him even more than I thought possible.

Ignoring his previous question, I murmured, "This fantasy…it's not just about the sex, is it? It's the whole experience. The birdsong and serenity. The peace where no other humans exist." I smiled softly, blending seriousness with joviality. "If I didn't know you, I'd say this was based on Tarzan. After all, you're a complicated man who not many understand. You have the uncanny ability to befriend any animal you come across, and you prefer to keep the entire human race as far away from you as possible. I don't know how I didn't see it before." I looked him up and down, drinking in the wild perfection. "You're Tarzan."

He let out a deep chuckle, ducking to his haunches to scratch the cat under its chin. "When you label it, yes, it does seem that way." His eyes glittered as he studied me intently, lingering on my pussy and nipples. "You do make a delectable Jane. Wasn't she a virgin? An innocent young girl who caught the attention of a man raised by animals?"

"She fell in love with him the instant she saw him."

"And he with her." His eyes never left mine, making me wet, fluttering my heart, clenching my entire body with need.

"And they had copious amounts of sex," I breathed.

"Filthy creatures."

I licked my lips. "Obsessed."

"Addicted." His hands continued to stroke the jaguar. Long, strong fingers that had been on me, in me, everywhere on me. I found every part of him terrifyingly tempting.

Desire thickened the air between us.

Our skin sparked with chemistry that never stopped tormenting us. My mouth begged to be on his. My body pleaded to be filled by him.

The only problem was, we still had a guest.

One with big teeth.

Swallowing down my need, I moved hesitantly toward Sully and the cat.

Sully gave me a gentle nod as I dared to hold out my hand to the jaguar. The cat sniffed me, licked me once with its sandpaper tongue, then continued to purr thanks to Sully's petting.

"All this…" My voice scratched with lust. I cleared my throat, adding, "This fantasy: the animals, the jungle, even the treehouse, it's all similar to Tarzan…apart from one thing."

"Oh, and what's that?" Sully asked smoothly.

"A gorilla. You're missing a—"

A branch snapping whirled me around just as a silver and black monkey appeared from the shadowy leaves all around us.

A damn gorilla.

I laughed under my breath as the primate dropped from the trees and thudded against the deck. The jaguar didn't flinch or try to kill it. Its eyes closed in utmost contentment beside Sully.

The gorilla blinked at me, its long eyelashes catching the sunlight and its silvery black hair so fine and soft. A female. Not fully grown, inquisitive and sweet, studying me as curiously as I studied her.

How did Sully do it?

How did he conjure a creature just from code?

How did he get every nuance of her movements and every filament of her hair so perfect?

I locked my knees as the gorilla reached for my necklaces, her black hands heavily padded for jungle climbing and thick with power. The beads and shells clacked as she tugged one of the cords.

I removed it and handed it to her.

She grunted and dropped to her butt, studying her new possession.

Sully stood, leaving his hand on the jaguar's head. "You're going to ask if I summoned that gorilla, aren't you?" He smirked. "That I elaborated on the Tarzan theme and deliberately cyphered her to prove you're correct. That I have a thing for a childhood storybook."

I padded toward him, awed by the two animals just happily hanging out with us. "You have to admit, it's rather coincidental."

"Or the fantasy felt what you were thinking and delivered."

"Can a computer program do that?"

Sully shrugged, his naked chest once again distracting me with his chiselled strength. "Programs evolve. There are updates and new editions."

"So, yes or no?" I rested my palm over his heart. He shuddered at our connection, hissing between his teeth as electricity fired between us.

"I don't know." His tongue ran over his bottom lip. "Along with the creatures I created previously, I tweaked a line of code to create animals known to be found in jungles. I didn't state what animals. I just let the program decide." Grabbing my wrist, he jerked me closer.

It was my turn to hiss as his body pressed against mine. Hot and slightly tacky with sweat and hard in all the right places. "Think of another animal, Jinx. Let's see if you have the ability to summon an aardvark or a buffalo."

My mind went blank as he tipped my chin up with his knuckle, holding me still as he looked deep into my eyes. "You know I love you more than any other person, before or since. You know that I always will, but I don't think you fully understand *why* I fell in love with you in the first place."

I swayed in his control, my breasts growing heavy and a

trickle of want on my inner thigh. "Why?" My question was a gentle puff of air as the jaguar stood, stretched, and leapt off the deck, vanishing stealthy and sleek into the trees.

"I fell for you because of Skittles." His lips pressed against mine. He kissed me slow and deep, distracting me, corrupting me. I clung to him, opening wider, permitting him to guide me wherever he wanted.

Pulling away, I asked breathlessly. "Skittles?"

"She showed me who you were beneath the beauty, the fight, the goddess I'd purchased. Because of her trust in you—when she'd never trusted anyone—I knew without a shadow of a doubt that you were *good*. Kind. The exact opposite of what I'd become." He kissed me again, his tongue slipping past my lips and completely stealing me from conversation.

The deck shuddered as the gorilla followed the jaguar and abandoned us to our lust. Sully backed me toward the railing where vines dangled like living ribbons.

With our tongues dancing and bodies burning for more, he pressed me against the balustrade. One hand remained on my waist, kneading me, pulling my hips into his, but the other let me go, the slight breeze of air hinting he did something I couldn't see.

Breathing hard, I nipped his bottom lip, needing to know.

His eyes glowed sapphires as he wrapped a vine around my wrist, trapping me.

The moment he'd tied me, he stepped back and raked his hands through his hair. "You did say I could do anything to you, correct?"

I tugged against the vine; the snug softness belied the strength behind the creeper. It was just us. No more cats or gorillas. No more talk about programs and true love.

Just drowning attraction and blistering sexual need.

I swallowed and nodded.

Sully growled low in his chest. "I'll make this good for you, Jinx. So fucking good." With slightly shaking hands, he removed his loincloth, throwing it over the side of the deck. It fluttered through the branches, leaving Sully stunningly naked.

His cock hung heavy and hard. His balls tucked against his body in need. His flat stomach rippled with shallow breaths. Crowding into me, he grabbed the vine by my other wrist and once again, used it to secure me.

He didn't speak as he climbed onto the banister and tugged at vines hanging above us, pulling them lower from their tangles to drape a few around me. Bits of bracken and dried leaves rained around us as he reached for me and plucked me from the deck.

I couldn't move my arms as he held me high enough to position my leg through a looped hanging vine before repeating with my other. "Balance." He let me go, leaving the two vines around my thighs to hold my weight as I swung with my legs parted.

It took effort to stay in place, especially with my wrists tied, and my stomach clenched as he once again jumped onto the railing and tugged another few vines to waist level. With sure hands and quick calculations, he reclined me onto the new loops, ensuring three thick foliage ropes cradled my back and neck.

My hair cascaded behind me; my necklaces and anklets tinkled quietly with my every sway.

Only once he'd added vines to my ankles, leaving the vines swinging from the treetops above and splaying my legs open did he step back to inspect my imprisonment.

I squirmed in the bondage, testing the parameters and seeking a way free.

He groaned as my legs scissored, then splayed wide thanks to the vines keeping me trapped. His hand dropped to his cock, his fingers lashing tight around his erection. "You look positively divine."

I struggled again, trying to keep my legs closed, all while the swinging strength of the vines parted them, revealing every private part of me.

He'd effectively made a sex swing out of the jungle.

He'd lashed and looped me so I had nowhere to go, no way to run from whatever he was about to do.

Cinta sprang back into power in my veins. Lust shoved aside words and worries, drenching me in debilitating desire. If I wasn't supported by the vines, I would've puddled to his feet and *begged* him to touch me.

His stare was a visceral thing.

The way he masturbated while feasting on my prone body made the coils of a climax begin in my belly.

Touch me.

Fuck me.

Please!

"Want something, Eleanor?" He jerked himself harder. "You're growing wetter by the second, so you can't deny it."

I nodded, desperation making me insane. "You. I want you."

"How? How do you want me?"

I watched him jerking off. The brutalising squeeze, the harsh punishment. He'd never been a gentle lover, and I wanted it as hard as he delivered.

"I want that." I arched my chin at his cock, my vision turning hazy. "I want you to touch me like that."

"Where?" he growled.

"*Everywhere.*"

My skin flushed as his gaze turned midnight and flashed with violent lust. "Your wish is my command, Goddess Jinx." Stepping into me, he slammed to his knees between my wide legs. "Fuck, I'm going to enjoy this."

Chapter Twelve

ELEANOR WAS ALL MY weaknesses in one.

Her taste as my tongue entered her pussy.

Her moans as I worshipped her.

Her jerks as I inserted two fingers.

Her scent as I pushed her toward another release.

All of her.

Every mewl, every smile, every touch, every moment had the power to kill me in the best way possible. I would die a happy man if I was permitted to spend the rest of my life right here on my knees before my exquisite wife.

She swung in the vines, the natural strength of the creepers holding her at the perfect height for me to feast. Withdrawing my fingers, I planted my hands on either of her thighs, pushing her wider apart.

She cried out as the vines pulled while I pushed, spreading her so I could witness every fold, glisten, and secret. Her head tipped back as I bent my neck and sucked on her clit.

"Fuck, *Sully.*" She spasmed as I licked my way down to her entrance.

Her taste was a mix of both of us. A blend of prior pleasure and a carnal pledge of our marriage.

"I can't...I'm-I'm—" Her voice echoed with pain and pleas. "Please, Sully. Let me—"

I drove my tongue deeper into her, my nose buried on her clit, my entire face between her legs.

She didn't stand a chance.

I drove her up and shoved her over.

She came on my mouth, her orgasm twitching her in the vines, over and over as her body splintered and shattered.

I climbed to my feet before she'd finished, wiping away the slickness on my chin and notching my hips between her legs. My cock stood to full attention as I rubbed myself on her, gathering up her wetness, teasing both of us.

She moaned and struggled to raise her head, slumped and sated in the vines. She blinked with hooded eyes, watching where my cock pleasured both of us. "Sully..."

"Need something else?" I pressed harder, making her swing, bringing her to a stop with my hands on her breasts. The shells and beads draping over her beautiful flesh tried to hide her decency. Grabbing them, I yanked them over her head, allowing them to fall in a shower of discarded jewellery to the deck.

She flinched as a cord broke, scattering its contents and bouncing beads through the slats of the bamboo, disappearing to the forest floor below.

She'd never looked more sublime. Coffee tangled hair all loose around her, her arms spread and bound, her body defying gravity at the perfect height for me to plunge inside. I wondered what position our bodies were in back at Hawksridge Hall. Did I have her on the bed? On the floor? Had our desire caused our tethers to untie, in which case we could be in the fucking corridor by now.

But I didn't care.

The only thing I cared about was being inside this woman. Again and again and *again*.

Fisting myself, I pushed her forward, loving the pendulum effect of her trapped and swinging. She bit her bottom lip as her momentum brought her back to me.

Using gravity to do my work, I angled my cock and waited for her to return to me.

Her mouth opened wide as she swung directly onto my cock, sinking me inside her, inserting me to the hilt in one rock.

"Holy *shit*." I groaned, my knees locking against the bands of pleasure shooting down my legs.

Eleanor gasped, her chest panting with pure pleasure. "Oh, my God."

My fingernails dug into her hips, pulling her harder into me, needing to crawl inside her.

And she let me.

She had no choice. This was my true fantasy. Having her completely at my mercy. To take my time with her. To torment. To control. To own.

With my hands on her knees, I pushed her forward, drawing her down my length, leaving glistening desire covering me.

She shuddered as I pushed until she hovered on my tip. Her pussy spread, welcoming me to take her deeper. My breath caught. I couldn't move as a lashing orgasm spiralled up my legs and throbbed in my balls.

It would be so easy to come. Too easy. But I wanted to drive both of us insane first.

Allowing her to fall toward me, I groaned as her body enveloped mine, slick and warm.

She whimpered as I jerked her closer, locking us together until my hip bones dug into her inner thighs. "Feel that? Every piece of me is inside you."

She nodded. "I feel it."

"Like it?"

"*Love* it."

I pushed again, drawing her away, wincing at the coolness left behind after the sensual heat of her body. "Do you miss me when I'm not inside you?"

Her forehead furrowed in concentration as I let her swing forward, gliding down my cock again. "Yes."

"Do you dream of me when I'm asleep beside you?"

"Yes."

"What do you dream about?"

She licked her lips, her breath catching as I pushed and pulled. Standing still, I used the vines to fuck her without moving my hips.

"I...I dream about our first time in Euphoria. The cave and the fire and the blizzard, and how you said I was yours, even then."

"You were born mine." I fucked her slowly, tantalizingly.

"I know."

Her swing increased as I pushed and pulled, watching the graphic show of my body vanishing into hers, over and over.

We lost ourselves to torment.

Our breaths turned shallow with the rapidly building need to come. Her skin flushed as I pushed her to the very tip of my cock, holding her away.

Her spread legs trembled while only the tiniest fraction of me remained inside her. "Sully...please."

"Please what?"

"Please have me. All of me."

I swallowed the possession racing in my blood. "I already have. Every moment of our life together, I have you."

"You know what I mean."

I forced a smile through foggy lust. "What do you mean, dirty wife?"

"I mean fuck me. Hard. I want—"

I drove deep and quick, shutting her up, giving her what she asked for.

I did it again and again.

Using the vines and my own power, I ensured her body would feel every inch of mine for days to come.

"*Yes.*" She bowed in the creepers, submitting to everything I gave her.

She looked fucking amazing.

So trusting and loving. So sure in my affection and commitment to her.

It was that part that undid me the most.

I had her utterly at my mercy, but I didn't need to because her trust gave me every power over her. Just like my trust in her was the most sacred and precious thing I'd ever done.

She'd taught me the meaning of the word.

She'd set me free.

I fucked her harder.

I couldn't help it.

My love overflowed into violence.

Eleanor would always consume my thoughts.

From her regal bearing with her invisible crown to her debased and spread-eagled on my cock, I loved every facet of her.

She shivered as I suddenly shoved her forward and let her go, allowing gravity to pierce her onto me, sliding us together in a fierce impale.

"Oh, my God—" She gulped as her entire body fissured with longing.

The suddenness.

The tightness.

I struggled to stay standing. I buckled and clung to her,

bending over her prone body to capture her mouth.

She moaned into my kiss, her tongue as eager as mine, her lips sweet and soft while mine attacked hers with rapidly dwindling control.

While I kissed her, my hips began to rock, fucking her the old-fashioned way, cursing the vines as they kept her weightless and swinging away from my thrusts.

I growled into her mouth and grabbed her breasts, holding her in place while I picked a punishing pace to rut into her.

Our kiss turned into nips and gasps.

Our flesh smacking.

Our lust evolving into a fierce, ferocious master.

I'd meant to prolong this. I'd wanted her in tears and begging for a release, but I couldn't wait. I needed to spurt inside this woman. I needed that sweet connection of afterward.

Kissing her harder, I wrapped my arms around her and drove short, sharp, and punishingly into her.

She lost the ability to kiss me back. Her breasts bounced against my chest. The vines shuddered with my every rock. Her entire attention turned inward as I set off the chain reaction of her release.

Her every muscle clenched as I fucked her.

Her mouth opened wide and her legs snapped straight as she tumbled from coherent queen into a clenching, orgasming animal.

And I followed her.

I pulled away and used the swing of the vines to add depth to my thrusts. Pushing and pulling, thrusting and fucking, driving every inch deep within her to come.

My head fell back on the first splash.

My belly convulsed and my balls squeezed in pleasure that threatened to snap my legs in half.

Blackness descended over my vision, blocking out the fantasy as I focused entirely on Eleanor and the incredible link we shared.

It wiped me clean.

It deleted who I'd been before her.

I jerked as aftershocks kept ricocheting up my legs, blinking back stars as I glanced down at my wife.

Her grey gaze smoked with sated satisfaction. Her lips tilted into a lazy smile. "Welcome back." Her body hung comfy and loose in the vines.

I winced as she wriggled, sending another few shards of bliss down my cock. "You broke me."

She laughed gently, her inner muscles once again fisting me in delicious ways. "I think you broke both of us."

"I wanted that to last longer."

"No reason it can't." Her legs struggled to close, fighting against the vines' entrapment. "*Cinta* isn't done with us yet."

I grinned, looking at where we stayed joined, drinking in the perfection of everything that I'd gained by earning her love. "You're right. We have plenty of time to play."

"We're on holiday, after all." She smiled.

"When you put it that way…" Gathering her close, I tugged her out of the vines' embrace. "I know the perfect place for another playground."

Tumbling into my arms, Eleanor didn't object as I scooped her from the deck and marched toward the small bamboo walkway leading deeper into the trees.

This was an illusion. Well fabricated and carefully coded.

A place of absolute freedom.

A wonderland where reality wasn't welcome, sex was unbelievable, and every moment with my wife was the ultimate fantasy.

And I wasn't finished with her yet.

Chapter Thirteen

SULLY STAYED TRUE TO his word.

He had the perfect playground. The entire jungle was his domain and dynasty. Taking me by the hand, he led me from the treehouse, down animal tracks in dense foliage, through a crystal clear stream complete with tadpoles and a family of leopard cubs playing in the grasses, to a cave almost entirely covered by lichen and low hanging jasmine vines.

Keeping our fingers entwined, we explored the dark tomb and travelled deeper into the earth's belly until no natural light encroached and the fairy-tale sparkle of glow-worms pinpricked the blackness.

There, he took me over a moss-covered rock.

Got on his knees and spread me over his lap.

And kissed me for hours as we slowly grew drowsy from our lovemaking.

I had no idea how much time had passed—whether it was dawn in Hawksridge Hall or if we still had hours before the Hawks expected us to join them for breakfast, but our time in this place would always be remembered as one of the best times in Euphoria we'd shared.

Not because it'd been the most erotic but because we were both so at home here.

So at peace watching parrots of all colours, monkeys of all

shapes, and the shadows of elephants slinking on the horizon as we left the cave and strolled under stars that mimicked the glow-worms we'd just left behind.

So much life all around us—the reminder that no matter where we were or what form we currently inhabited, we were all connected in some way—virtual or real.

Sully stopped me as we broke the jungle and stood on a savannah with giraffes in the distance and a pride of lions growling at the crescent moon. I looked at my husband as he slowly stroked my wrist, his fingers hovering over the patch of skin that would terminate this illusion.

After his previous renditions of Euphoria, with the absolute entrapment of a person's mental faculties until they fell asleep, he'd updated the code and added a way out without having to be unconscious.

I shivered as he brought my hand up and kissed the area on my wrist. "Ready to go back?"

"Not really."

His head tipped up, a lazy smile on his gorgeous face. "Aren't you tired?" He chuckled. "I admit, I need to rest so I'm not a grumpy bastard at breakfast or a gloating asshole for having the best wife a man could hope for."

"I'm pretty sure Jethro would argue that *he* has the best wife. Everyone thinks they have the best."

"And they do. Because it's true…to them." He straightened, pressing a simple kiss to my cheek. "But you're still the best out of anyone."

I laughed quietly, freezing as a giraffe stopped munching on a tree and threw a spooked look our way. "You're such a charmer."

"And you're a witch. There's no other explanation for how much I adore you." Pinching the skin of my wrist, he smiled gently. "See you back at Hawksridge Hall, Eleanor."

I held my breath as the illusion switched from solid and true, to hazy and obscured by smoke. The firmness of soil beneath my bare feet faded. The wonder of a tropical jungle was suddenly gone. Everything vanished, leaving me in a world of white before a quick hiss of static and the sharp bump of reality deposited me back into England and the impressive history-rich suite we'd been given.

I gasped as embroidered carpets replaced dirt and an instant chill found me as I stood naked at the foot of the bed, the bathrobe belt still latched around my ankle, keeping me tied to the four-poster.

Sully stood beside me, his fingers pinching his own wrist. His eyes still saw the virtual world I'd just left, but a few breaths later with a full-body jolt, he joined me in England. Blinking away our fantasy and giving me a sexy smirk, he murmured, "At least we're still in the room and not on the lawn."

I smiled. "I can imagine that would've earned a few side-eyes at breakfast."

Stepping into me, he wrapped his arms tight around me, granting me much-needed body heat. "You're cold. Let's get into bed." Kissing me, he let me go before ducking to untie me. His eyes feasted on my nakedness as he freed me. "You have bruises." Touching the finger shadows on my hips, he bit his bottom lip. "I didn't mean—"

"Bruises are a symbol of a great night together." I captured his hand, holding it against my hip. "I would've been disappointed if you'd been gentle."

"I don't think I'll ever be able to be gentle with you. I need you too violently." Standing, he scooped me off my feet and carried me to the bed. The barely noticeable limp he still had from everything Drake had done to him came and went.

Ripping back the thick coverlets, he dropped me into the centre, then climbed in after me.

The novelty of having heavy blankets instead of a thin sheet was strange but comforting. I sighed in happiness as he curled around me, keeping me warm and safe.

Shifting together, we removed our eye lenses and earbuds and discarded them on the bedside table. The hall creaked as a gust of wind disrupted ancient windowpanes and wafted thick tapestries. Thank goodness Sully and the bed were warm. Otherwise, I'd freeze.

Yawning, I slid quicker into exhaustion than I'd planned. I'd wanted to ask Sully again what he'd done to Drake. After five years of not wanting to know, I had a sudden need to understand.

But Sully had changed the subject in our hallucination and we'd never returned to it. I knew the topic was mostly off-limits. That what he did was between him and his brother. But I couldn't help wondering, especially now I'd seen the relationship between Sully's cyphered animals and his commands.

Had he used that connection to break Drake's mind? Had he enlisted the help of animals to tear him into pieces—both figuratively and literally?

I tensed, imagining what it would've been like to watch a man like Drake—a man who'd embraced a heinous calling to torment, steal, and pillage—be massacred by the very animals he'd chosen to hurt.

Sully nuzzled into the back of my neck, his breath evening out in peace. His serenity added another layer to my tiredness, and I slipped closer to sleep.

My question didn't matter.

What was done was done.

It was in the past.

All that mattered now was the man cocooning me in trusted arms. A man who'd delivered passion and pleasure. A man I would never stop loving.

I slept.

* * * * *

"Wow, you didn't waste any time." I grinned as I padded from the bathroom wrapped in a fluffy towel, steam chasing me as I brushed my long hair. I'd had the shower as hot as I could bear it, standing beneath the scalding rain before risking the chilly English morning.

Sully grinned, zipping up our shared suitcase where everything we'd brought with us had been stuffed back in ready for a return trip home. "After breakfast, we're leaving. Already arranged." Coming toward me, his five o'clock shadow trim and rakish and his body already dressed in slacks and navy shirt, he cupped my cheek. "I decided on a little detour, though."

"Oh?"

"Philippines." He kissed me before pointing at the jeans, white knitted jumper, and teal scarf laid out on the bed. "Spoke to Cal who convinced me to check it out. So dress, darling wife, before I'm tempted to load another fantasy."

I laughed under my breath as he patted my ass and pushed me toward my chosen wardrobe. Dropping my towel, I flushed with pleasure as Sully jerked and swallowed hard.

The bruises he'd given me last night had bloomed into a richer colour, marking me entirely as his. Only we knew where we'd gone and what we'd done. Only we had a superpower to teleport to wherever we damn well wanted and indulge in raw, toe-curling eroticism.

"Goddammit, will I ever get enough of you?" He reached out to cup my breast, but I swatted him away, slipping into a white lace bra.

"You'll have to. I don't know the exact time, but I'm guessing we're probably running late for breakfast."

He shrugged. "It's only nine a.m. Jethro said between nine and nine-thirty is fine."

Stepping into a matching set of knickers before pulling on the jeans, I threw him a look. "By the way, you can't drop the fact that we're travelling to the Philippines instead of Indonesia and not elaborate." Slipping into the jumper, I waited for him to fill me in.

He cleared his throat. "I miss Pika and Skittles but...I also miss Cal and Jess. If they're having so much fun over there, I thought we might as well go see what all the fuss is about."

"Really?"

He smiled. "I know that won't be an issue for you, seeing as you were born to travel."

"I was born to find you."

"Yes, well, you found me. And now we have another adventure to look forward to. Together." Taking my hand, he pulled me toward the door. "Now, come along, England is too cold for my taste. The sooner we say goodbye, the sooner we can chase the sun."

"And you call yourself a good friend." I tutted as Sully escorted me down the long corridor with its medieval flair of decoration. "Leaving the day after we arrive."

"Jethro knows who I am. He knows I have a small tolerance of people—no matter if I like them or not. He can sense it."

"Sense it how? Nila said something similar last night when we visited the stables."

Sully waited until I clutched the banister of the sweeping staircase before descending with me. "He's an Empath. Also known as HSP—Highly Sensitive Person."

"What exactly does that mean?"

"It means he's in-tune with a sense all humans have. His is just more developed, and he can't shut it off. It's caused a lot of complications in his world." He smiled as we reached the bottom level. "In fact, I bet you he'll know *exactly* what our plans are the moment we sit at the table."

I laughed, looking up at him and admiring the shadow and sun highlighting his lovely face. "What do you bet me?"

His blue eyes glistened. "An orgasm?"

I pursed my lips, weighing up the bet. "Make it two and you have yourself a deal." I held out my hand.

Sully chuckled but shook. "You've already lost, Eleanor, but deal. I expect to collect my two orgasms the moment we touch down in the Philippines."

"That can be arranged."

"I'll hold you to that." Sharing another laugh, rich with affection and happiness, we followed the twisting, gothic corridor and entered the sun-dappled drawing room.

Sullivan

Chapter Fourteen

"GOOD MORNING." JETHRO GLANCED from me to Eleanor as he stood respectfully from the table where he and Nila waited. His amber eyes narrowed and the tell-tale sign that he was listening with a sense other than his ears hinted I was about to win the bet before we'd even sat down.

However, with a knowing smile, Jethro returned to his seat and waved elegantly at the large spread waiting to be devoured. "Please, join us. I assume you two *slept* well." He smirked before he could wipe his face back to politeness.

He couldn't fool me.

We'd gone through too many trials, errors, and confessions to hide his gift.

Giving him a mocking bow, I grinned. "It seems daylight has reminded you of your manners, Hawk." Guiding Eleanor to the table, I held out her chair and waited until she sat before sitting beside her.

Nila rolled her eyes, answering me on behalf of her husband. "Kite forgot to keep his barriers up last night. He listened to things that weren't his to hear."

Jethro chuckled. "Nila is quite right. I do owe you an apology. Especially you, Eleanor. You don't know me, and I hope I didn't make too bad a first impression."

Eleanor shook her head, her gorgeous chocolate hair a dark

cascade against the white of her jumper. "Not at all. I hope it's okay, but Sully mentioned a little of your...expertise?"

"Disease, more like it." Jethro took Nila's hand sitting on top of the table. "Until Nila came along, of course."

Nila smiled gently before remembering her hostess duties. "Please, tuck in. Your security staff advised that you're vegetarian, so I ensured all our fare this morning is edible by all of us. Our eggs are free-range from hens that basically run this estate, and the milk is from our almond grove."

I bowed my head. "That's very considerate."

"Not at all. I've been leaning more that way myself lately." Nila shuddered. "I've seen our gamekeeper skinning rabbits and deer, and I have to say, it makes me queasy after seeing them happily living in our woods before ending up dead on our plates."

Jethro winced, picking up on the truth of Nila's admittance. Clearing his throat, he glanced at Eleanor. "Did you have a pleasant evening? The room wasn't too drafty while you, eh...scratched the itch you were both suffering from dancing last night?"

Eleanor choked on a mouthful of orange juice.

Nila swatted her husband.

I just laughed. "Instead of coming up with your own conclusions of what we got up to last night, I can tell you in explicit detail. You'll never be able to guess."

"Oh, no need." Jethro chuckled. "I have a rather cohesive answer just from looking at you two."

"Let's put you to a test, shall we?" I steepled my hands on the table, watching him carefully. "For old time's sake."

"I didn't like your tests then, and I'm not interested now." Hawk scowled. "You'd think you were writing a book on my condition—"

"I did actually. I wrote all your symptoms down—the ones you shared with me, especially in those earlier days—and asked my head scientist, Peter Beck, to see if there was a way to give you distance from other's emotional broadcasts."

"And?" Jethro cleared his throat. "Did you find anything, or did you just formulate that abysmal drug you gave my father to shut me down completely?"

I sat back, guilt flaring over that.

Eleanor gave me a quick look, sensing the nasty history and my role in it.

"He lied to me." I shrugged. "He said you were self-harming

because you couldn't cope anymore. I tried calling you—"

"I was self-harming because I'd fallen in love with Nila and couldn't unscramble her love for a monster like me and the hate my father had for her. I was being split apart. I couldn't hear myself think over the evilness of my family and the pureness of the woman I'd fallen for."

Nila interrupted gently. "Is this really breakfast talk?" Throwing Eleanor an apologetic smile, she added, "Jethro wasn't, eh, well when we first found each other. He—"

"I hurt her unforgivably," Jethro snapped, glaring at the diamond collar that sparkled around Nila's neck. The choker had looked stunning last night with her ball gown, yet here, while she wore a simple cream shirt and jeans, it drenched the table with rainbows full of wealth and yesteryears debts.

"It all worked out in the end," I said. "You know I didn't intentionally try to break you guys apart."

"You what?" Eleanor asked, her eyebrows flaring high. "They broke up because of a drug you made?"

"No." Jethro shook his head. "I take full blame. I sent her away to protect her. My father threatened me, as per usual, and gave me some pills that he said would help. They drowned out every part of me and only left the son my father wanted. It caused struggles between Nila and me."

"But I snapped him out of it before it was too late," Nila said softly. "And he hasn't taken another drug since."

"Which is why you'll have to let me assess you one day," I muttered. "So I know how to help other HSPs."

"Tell them to fall in love with someone who has their back." Jethro ran a hand through his salt and pepper hair. "That's it." His tension faded as he brought the conversation back around to me and Eleanor instead of himself and Nila. "And don't think I'm not aware you changed the subject so I wouldn't give away details of your busy night. Not very guest-like behaviour, Sullivan." He narrowed his eyes, studying me, then Eleanor. "Bondage? Something to do with tying your wife—"

"Oh, my God." Eleanor spluttered. "How on earth could you possibly know that?"

"Ugh, he's incorrigible." Nila rolled her eyes, passing Eleanor a plate of roasted portobello mushrooms. "Ignore him. I do."

"You do not. You indulge my every whim. That's why I'm far too free with my 'abilities' these days."

"Yes well, Kes is starting to show signs, and if he sees his father acting like some gypsy fortune teller, he'll believe it's normal to go around telling people their own thoughts."

Jethro shrugged. "I hid my entire life and look how fucked up I was. If he's like me, then I don't want him to have to hide. I want him to know he doesn't have to."

Nila sighed, true love shining in her dark gaze. "I agree. It's just hard to explain when he runs up to the cook and says she's overweight because she's still grieving her cat's death two years ago."

Sully cut in. "You're saying your son has inherited Jethro's traits?"

Nila sighed, passing around a dish of wilted spinach in olive oil and sea salt. "I'm not sure. Some days, I swear he's exactly like Jet. Others, I think it was just a lucky guess. He's a normal boisterous child, but there is a quiet listener inside him too."

Jethro helped himself to buttery baguette. "We'll deal with it if he is like me. Least Emma is normal."

"Normal means nothing these days," I said, sipping a full-bodied espresso that one of the hall's staff placed in front of me. "I don't think there is such a thing as normal. If there is, I haven't found one in my line of work."

"How is work going?" Jethro asked. "Any new breakthroughs in modern medicine?"

"Always. Whether or not the population is ready to accept it is another question."

"How do you sit on drugs you know will work when you can't get it past all the bureaucratic red tape?" Jethro asked.

I set my coffee cup down. "I have my ways of trickling it into the marketplace."

A squeal sounded, heralding two little cyclones as they dashed into the drawing room. A boy and a girl—perfect replicas of their aristocratic parents. Their outward appearance was finely dressed, but their screams of joy as they played chase around the table hinted they were wild with energy and freedom.

Growing up in a massive hall like Hawksridge would cultivate fiercely independent and well-rounded offspring.

Emma crashed into her mother's side, her mouth open for air as she scrambled onto Nila's lap, kicking at her brother as he tried to tickle her. "No. Safe. Safe!"

Kes, the older of the two, cackled and pulled her hair gently. "Nowhere is safe. Cheater!"

Jethro scooped him round the middle, hauling him onto his

own lap. "Say hello to friends of ours. Sullivan and Eleanor."

Kes blushed as he caught my stare then Jinx's. He calmed eerily quickly in his dad's embrace, almost as if he could sense the crimes I'd done in the past and the type of man I'd been before Eleanor changed me for the better.

Slowly, he nodded. "Hello."

The way he watched with such dedication and knowing hinted he had inherited Jethro's gift, after all. Only time would tell to what degree.

"Hello," I said. "Having fun playing tag?"

"Not tag." He shook his head importantly. "Hunting. She's the hare. I'm the hound."

"Hares are faster than hounds." I smiled.

Emma clapped her hands. "Yay!"

"Yeah, but hounds can sniff stuff," Kes retorted.

"Hares can box and kick." I grinned as Jethro's son chewed his bottom lip, digesting such things.

"Em won't kick me hard. She won't dare."

Emma wriggled free of Nila's hug and bolted out of the drawing room. "Byeeeeee!"

"Hey!" Kes leaped out of Jethro's lap and galloped after her, leaving a wake of silence as their heavy footfalls faded down the endless corridors.

"They're adorable." Eleanor smiled. "Do you only have the two?"

Nila nodded. "Yes. Two is all we can handle. I'm sorry they're little heathens. I'd hoped the ball last night would've tired them out, but they're bundles of energy. They won't calm down until we take them for a ride."

"You can join us if you want," Jethro said softly. "I have horses you can borrow."

I glanced at Eleanor. Riding a horse to me was not enticing; however, if she wanted to, I would do whatever she requested. Catching my raised eyebrow, she shook her head.

"I'm happy just watching." Eleanor nodded. "Thanks, though."

"And besides, you have a plane to catch." Jethro chuckled under his breath. "I've been trying to guess where you're going, but I haven't been able to pinpoint. Tropical, no doubt. You both detest the cold."

"How did you—" Eleanor frowned. "How do you know? How does it work?"

Nila rolled her eyes again as she stabbed a blood-red strawberry with her fork, waiting for Jethro to enlighten Jinx. "Go on, you might as well spill, now that you've made a spectacle of yourself."

Jethro chuckled. "You pretend to be pissed at me but you can't lie that you're enjoying the openness of this conversation, Needle. That you're wary of sharing too much but grateful that Sully has been there from the beginning and isn't going to judge."

Nila nodded, leaning over to squeeze Jethro's hand. "Right as always."

Sharing an intimate moment with his wife, Jethro dropped his gaze before sitting back and locking eyes with Eleanor. "In answer to your question, it's not really something I can explain. I just...know. I look at you, and I feel cold. That isn't because *I'm* cold but because I'm guessing *you* are. I'm sitting in my own home where I'm happy and content, yet, I suddenly have a hankering for travel and turquoise seas. Two things that have never interested me in the slightest. When I was younger, I confused those feelings for my own. I fed on the emotions of cruelty because that was what I was raised in and what I believed came from my own heart. But I can keep the two separate now. I no longer need to numb the feeling of say needing to travel, or to grab another jumper to ward off the chill because that isn't me. It's you." He laughed quietly. "I also feel a thread of exhaustion from whatever indulgences you got up to last night." Holding up his hand, he added, "Oh, and there's a vein of embarrassment too, so whatever you got up to, it was frisky enough to make you blush in my company."

Eleanor's cheeks burned. "Your wife is right. You sound like a gypsy fortune teller."

"I suppose if my enterprise of diamonds fails, I could earn my keep that way." Jethro laughed.

I chuckled, squeezing Eleanor's knee under the table. "I believe I won our bet, Jinx."

Eleanor narrowed her eyes. "In the words of Kes Hawk...cheater."

"I didn't cheat. I just had insider knowledge." I chuckled. "But I'm still going to make you pay."

Eleanor blushed harder. "I'm not discussing orgasm payments at the breakfast table."

Jethro burst into laughter.

Nila giggled and kindly changed the subject. "Do you have

children of your own?"

Eleanor rubbed at her flaming cheek, grateful for the topic switch. "No. We don't. And please don't say the politically correct 'Oh, I'm sorry'. Don't be. It's a personal choice."

"A joint decision." I squeezed Eleanor's knee again. "We currently have over four hundred rescues under our protection with more arriving every week. That is where our heart lies. With the abused, unwanted, and homeless."

"I love that." Nila smiled. "You get to nurture something that desperately needs it."

Eleanor nodded. "Give me any kind of creature, and I have an unbearable need to care and snuggle and protect. But give me a child, and I don't know what to do with it." She laughed gently. "I'm not maternal for my own kind."

Nila returned Eleanor's laugh. "I completely understand, especially now that I'm a mother, I can safely say that sometimes I look at wild animals and think they're so much better behaved than my own offspring. Even though they drive me loopy, I love them with everything that I am."

My mind turned inward, recalling the conversation Eleanor and I had shared two years or so into our marriage. I'd never once, in all my years, ever wanted a kid of my own. Why the hell would I want to add to the already overpopulated human race when I couldn't stand us as a species? My legacy and fortune had already been bequeathed to shelters and my own personal rescue charities, so I didn't need an heir to inherit.

It never occurred to me to have the conversation about children with my wife.

Our world was perfect. Nothing was missing.

But it'd been Cal who told me I should at least *ask* Eleanor. That it wasn't normal for a couple not to discuss the choice to breed or not.

It'd taken a few nights to get up the courage. What if Eleanor *did* want kids? Where did that leave us? The thought of putting her at risk with impregnation? Of watching her be in pain? I *despised* the thought of it. But I'd forced myself to ask on a particularly romantic evening on our deck overlooking Nirvana. A pair of macaws got frisky in a palm tree above our heads, giving me a sign to ask a troubling question.

I'd turned to Jinx, swallowed back my fear, and asked, "Do you want children, Eleanor?"

She'd frozen.

Our ease and drowsiness from a delicious dinner vanished as she bolted off her lounger and paced in front of me. Raking hands through her hair, she'd licked her lips and made me wait for an agonising few minutes.

I'd tried to read her.

Tried to figure out what the panic on her face meant. Did she desperately want them and didn't have the courage to tell me? Did she hate me for not asking sooner—

"Do *you* want kids?" she'd fired back, wringing her hands, her grey eyes dark with worry.

"I asked you first." I sat up, clasping my hands between my legs as I swung my feet to the deck. "Yes or no?"

She swallowed hard, forcing herself to be truthful. Her shoulders braced as she blurted, "It goes without saying that I want you to be happy, and if you want kids, then…I suppose we can discuss options like adoption or…I don't know." She sucked in a shaky breath. "But if I'm being honest about what *I* want, I have no interest in children of my own. None. Zip. Never." She stood trembling, waiting for me to stand and pad barefoot toward her.

Cupping her cheek, I nuzzled her nose with mine. "Well, thank fuck for that."

She almost puddled at my feet in relief. "You're saying you don't want them either?"

"Never in a million years."

"So you're fine, just us?"

"I'm fine with you." I kissed her hard. "I'm fine with our rescues and our animals and our family as it stands with Pika, Skittles, Cal, and Jess." I kissed her deeper. "I'm *more* than fine. I'm so fucking happy and it's all because of you. You're perfect, and I don't need or want anything else."

She kissed me back, shaking as she threw her arms around my shoulders. "I love you, Sully. I love that we're the same in all the ways that matter. Our animals are our children. Feathered, furred, scaled, and everything in between."

That night, we'd had sex that lasted until dawn. Reaffirming our vows. Acknowledging that we had no holes that needed to be filled or regrets we hadn't discussed.

We chose to stay committed to us. To our creatures. To our wonderful, idyllic life together.

If that was selfish, so fucking what? I believed by not having kids, we were helping the world with one less human to house.

Jethro interrupted my musing with his knowing stare. I sipped from my water glass, glowering back. "Quit reading me."

"But you're so interesting." He smirked as he chewed on a piece of cooked tomato. "Fascinating really. You're so unapologetically steadfast." He put his fork down. "When we first met, you were equally steadfast, just...in a much darker way."

"How so?" Eleanor piped up.

I threw her a look. "He means because of what I used to do."

"Before that. Before you started your side business unrelated to pharmaceuticals."

I froze. "You knew about that?"

Jethro shrugged. "I was aware you were doing something illegal, and you didn't feel bad about it. I don't know exactly what you were doing, because our talks were always by phone, and I don't pick up nearly as much just by someone's voice, but I was aware—almost to the day, in fact, when your thoughts weren't so...angry. You'd found an outlet toward the hate you felt toward people."

Eleanor tensed as I nodded slowly. "You're right. I did find an outlet by using the rules humans set for animal welfare against them. And you're also right that it did help the injustice in my mind. But it wasn't morally acceptable, and Eleanor helped me realise I couldn't keep exploiting any living creature."

Jethro raised his glass in a toast. "To our mutual personal growth thanks to our women."

"Here, here." I clinked my glass with his.

A companionable silence fell, a welcome reprieve to fill plates with delicious home-cooked fare and to indulge in a nutritious breakfast.

The Hawk children came dashing back in halfway through our meal. Emma had a dead mouse in her hand, and Kes had a falcon balancing on his forearm with its plumage ruffled and wings spread against the chaos of being tethered to a kid.

Jethro immediately put his knife and fork down, signalling Kes to bring him the falcon. "Did you go up to the mews without permission, Kes?"

The boy cringed as he passed his father the bird of prey. "They haven't flown today. I figured—"

"You know to wait for me."

"I know." He kicked the carpet. "But you guys are taking so *long*."

Nila patted her mouth with her napkin, standing elegantly

from the table. "Seeing as breakfast is interrupted, would you like to see an aerial dance?"

I pushed aside my plate and stood. I did my best not to focus on the string around the bird's foot or the fact that it was captive. It might have a good life with the Hawks. It might be fed and kept safe, but at the end of the day, it wasn't free to fly wherever it wanted.

It made me want to snatch the bird and cut the tether, but I balled my hands and kept my opinions about animal ownership to myself. I would *never* consider tying Pika or Skittles down. They spent time with us on their own accord, not because they were forced to.

"Sounds interesting," Eleanor said, her eyes also locked on the string around the bird's leg. "Lead the way."

Jethro brushed past me, his eyes on mine, knowing full well my disapproval as he held the falcon aloft.

In a neat file, all adults and children followed Jethro from the ancient looming hall into the watery English sunshine. There was no heat in the light. No humidity in the sky.

My skin prickled for both, and the urge to leave amplified, especially when Eleanor crushed against my side, and murmured, "Is it just me, or is that leash on the raptor driving you nuts?"

I sucked in a breath. "And that is why I fucking love you, Eleanor Sinclair." I couldn't help myself. I had to kiss her, so I did.

I kissed her in full view of Jethro and Nila Hawk while their two kids squabbled over who would throw the dead mouse.

At least the mouse was dead.

I wouldn't have been able to control myself if it'd been alive and facing torture by being thrown into the talons of a hunter.

With another guarded look my way, Jethro ordered Emma to throw the mouse as high as she could. At the same time, he swooped his arm up, boosting the falcon with its tawny feathers into the sky.

The bird screeched and shot after the mouse missile, snatching it from the sky in a blink.

Nila gathered Emma close, ducking on her haunches to watch the bird sail high and circle the estate. It would've been an impressive display if a leash wasn't trailing after the bird, its shackle ready to bind him back to earth always present.

"Goddammit." Jethro huffed beside me. "You're a real pain in my ass."

I stiffened, glancing at my friend. "What? Why am I a—"

"You know why." Pinching the bridge of his nose, he stomped away. "Nila, I'll be back. Ten minutes." Before she agreed, Jethro broke into a run, chewing up the manicured lawn in a hurry, heading toward the stone stables in the distance.

"What was that about?" Nila asked, leaving Emma to watch the falcon and coming to my side.

"No idea." I wrapped my arm around Eleanor. "All I can say is you married a strange man."

"Stop." Eleanor dug her elbow into my side. "Isn't it obvious?" She huffed as if I was stupid. "You've put feelings in his heart…about the bird. I can only guess how much it's driving you mad…which, in turn, has driven him mad." She looked at the swirling bird above our heads.

"Oh, my God, he's gone to the mews." Nila squinted into the sun after her husband.

"Are there more birds like the one above us?" I asked, tipping my head to follow the cruising path of the winged predator.

"There are seven or so, I think. Kestrels and hawks. Even an osprey."

We waited in silence as Jethro disappeared in the distance. Guilt crept over me for whatever my friend had felt. I hadn't meant to think of his animal care as subpar. I didn't want him to think I judged him for trapping birds…even though I did.

Eleanor was right.

I'm a shitty friend.

"I'll go after him. Apologise." I untangled my arm from around Eleanor. "I'll be right back."

"Wait." Eleanor grabbed my hand, looking at the sky.

Nila gasped and the two kids oohed and ahhed.

In the backdrop of blue sky and golden sun flew six sleek birds, slicing through the air as stealthy and as silently as death.

The thunder of hooves sounded beneath them, a black beast galloping with a man bareback.

No one spoke as Jethro pulled up his horse and leaped off while it was still moving, jogging a little with momentum before stopping beside his wife.

He gave me a sour look before pointing at the black horse who stood with its tail cocked and nostrils flared. It had no tack on. No bridle, no saddle, standing by its master of its own accord.

"That's acceptable to you, right?" Jethro muttered. "Wings wants to be here of his own free will. You're all right with that level of ownership?"

I fought a smile, knowing where this was going. Turned out his gift was still a curse in some ways. But today, it would benefit seven souls, so I was okay with that. I nodded, crossing my arms. "Yes, because that's not ownership, that's friendship."

Wings snorted, tossing his head before nuzzling the children out of the way and picking where they stood to munch on the grass.

Nila laughed and scratched the glossy creature, her attention still on the birds swirling above us, not leaving as if they knew they weren't permitted unless a signal was given.

Holding my stare, Jethro pulled a pair of banged-up barn scissors from his slacks pocket and raised his arm.

He whistled.

A flurry of feathers as the birds all dropped to land on him. Only one perched at a time and the rest shot back to the sky. With a glower at me, Jethro grabbed the dangling leash on a kestrel and snipped it free. He left the metal ring with identification details but tossed the leather string into the grass before raising his arm and shooting the bird back into the sky.

He repeated the process six more times.

A whistle, a bird, a snip, a throw until the discarded tethers looked like dead snakes in the grass. Only once each one was free did he whistle again, this one piercing and long. The signal to hunt.

The raptors dispersed and vanished, winging out in all directions, no leash, no belonging, just absolute freedom.

Jethro huffed and put the scissors back into his pocket. "Thanks to you, I could no longer keep them tied up in the mews. You and your strong opinions about animal welfare are a battering ram to someone like me, Sinclair."

I chuckled. "I didn't mean for you to release your entire flock."

"No, you didn't. But you're right. It's not fair to them. If they choose to live in the mews and come back, then fine. But if they leave, they should be protected by my identification and can go about their lives."

I held out my hand, waiting until he put his inside mine. "You're a good man, Hawk."

He shook his head, his scowl still present. "No, I'm not. But I'm trying to be."

Breaking apart, he scooped up Emma and placed her on his hip before grabbing the hand of his son. "Let's go for a walk." He bowed in Eleanor's direction before cocking his chin at me. "You owe me that after making me free my prized hunters."

"Fine." I grinned. "But then we have a plane to catch."

"Oh yes, the urge to chase heat and humidity. It's a constant hum inside you, Sullivan. It must be exhausting being you." He matched my grin. "Fine, yes. A walk and then you're free to leave. Free to return to your islands."

"In that case, a walk would be great." I took Eleanor's hand and let him lead the way.

We fell in step behind Jethro, heading toward the woodland and orchards.

Four adults.

Two children.

And one black horse, following as a friend because he wanted to.

Chapter Fifteen

I SNUCK INTO THE sunny drawing room at the front of the hall as Nila, Jethro, and Sully stood on the stoop, waiting for Radcliffe and his security team to bring the car around so we could return to the airport.

Our suitcase had been brought down from our room.

My ball gown and Sully's tux hung neatly on hangers with a thank-you note beside them. Our masks placed carefully on our bed that we'd barely slept in. The ballroom cleaned by excellent staff so no hint of a large event showed.

Our time was over here. We were ready to go.

It'd been a trip to remember, and I intended to keep a promise that I'd made to Nila as we walked back from the stables last night.

Sully and I had indulged in a different dimension. We'd travelled to a jungle and swung from vines in ecstasy. We had plenty of vials of *cinta* back at home, along with dozens and dozens of sensors to play in a virtual reality world.

The remaining two sets of eye lenses and earbuds that I'd brought weren't needed and the mostly full bottle of *cinta* could perhaps give Jethro and Nila a few memorable nights in this place like Sully and I had enjoyed.

Placing the box of Euphoria sensors on the crystal side table complete with a lamp in the shape of a tulip, I quickly scribbled another note.

Dear Nila,

Please accept this gift as a thank you for letting us attend your incredible masquerade and stay in your wonderful home. The sensors are to be worn by each of you, so you can see and hear within the VR creation. I'll send you the app you'll need to download on your phone so you can activate certain fantasies.
I've also included a bottle of cinta.
It's potent if you already feel lust for each other, and after watching you two together, I have no doubt there's much lust and love between you.
One drop should be enough to start.
Make sure you have no interruptions.
To end the fantasy, pinch your wrist for a few seconds or fall asleep.
If you have any questions, my inbox is always open.
I hope you have as much fun in Euphoria as we do.
Thanks again and stay in touch.
Eleanor.

Folding the note and tucking it under the unassuming box that granted such ecstasy, I glanced around Hawksridge Hall one last time, caught the flash of kestrel feathers as a freed raptor shot past the window, and headed back to my husband.
I looked forward to another adventure.
Another memory.
And smiled in joy, knowing we would go home soon.
Together.
Back to Pika and Skittles.
Back to tropical heat and turquoise seas.
Back to absolute paradise.

Jethro

I SAT IN BED, waiting for Needle to finish putting Kes and Emma to bed.

I'd attempted to help—we always did the bedtime routine together. However, I'd had to leave the final stages to Nila lately. Seeing as I couldn't seem to say no when they begged for another story. And another. And another.

I could feel their joy at spending time with us. The recited adventures weren't just stupid stories to them but true experiences they adored. They weren't doing it to drag out bedtime; they literally wanted to keep hanging out with their parents.

And I was fucking honoured by that.

So, of course, how the hell could I say no?

Hence why Nila did the final kisses and the terribly hard job of turning out their lights, ensuring the glowing heart lamp was on to protect them from the ghosts of Hawksridge Hall, and leaving them to bicker in the soft pink darkness while she tiptoed back to me.

I looked up as Nila entered.

She grinned, shutting the door behind her.

Three days had passed since our attempt at being social with the masquerade. Three days for me to get over my exhaustion of listening to so many different people, opinions, and right and wrong in everyone.

Three days since Sully and Eleanor had left.

And Nila had been cagey today, ever since she'd read an email from Eleanor and downloaded something on her phone.

"Alright, out with it." I glowered at my delicious wife as she kicked off her silken slippers and sat on her knees before me. Her dark hair hung in straight sheets, her chest rose and fell beneath her honey-coloured shirt.

Licking her lips, she sucked in a breath. "How are you feeling?"

"Me? Why? What's that got to do with whatever you're hiding?"

"I just want to know if you've recovered from the masq."

That was the thing about living with someone who got me. Who understood and accepted me unconditionally. I didn't need to hide, and that was the greatest fucking gift anyone could've given me.

This hall no longer had evil pouring through its brickwork. It had love and safety and utter happiness. Cut was gone. Daniel was rotting in Africa somewhere. Bonnie was ash. And Kes was regularly visited in his peaceful resting spot.

A lot of my family was dead, but those who deserved to stay alive were thriving.

Jasmine was happy.

My kids didn't have a heinous debt hanging around their necks.

There would be no more Debt Inheritance or death between my house and Nila's.

"I'm sufficiently revived. Why?" I took her hand, rubbing away the chill in her fingers. "What's going on?"

"I...have something."

"What something?"

"Eleanor gave it to me."

"Gave you what precisely?"

"I had to wait until today to get the link for the app she mentioned, but it's on my phone now. I've read her instructions. I know how to load Euphoria, and she's kindly included a few VR scenes that are ready to go."

I scowled. "What the hell is Euphoria. And VR?"

Nila shook in my hold, inhaling again. "It's one of Sullivan's creations."

I let her go, reclining against the pillows. "Oh no. I've had enough of his creations, thank you very much. If it's another drug, I'm not taking it. You, better than anyone, can understand why. Or are you forgetting what happened between us before the Third

Debt?"

She shook her head, her eyes flashing with pain as they always did when reminded about our screwed-up past. "It's not a drug. Well, it is, and it isn't."

"Not interested."

She huffed and grabbed her phone, her legs splicing apart before slipping gracefully beneath her. Tapping the screen, she brought up an app with palm trees and an emblem that said: 'Pleasure in Euphoria is euphoric'.

"This is an app that transports us to a different place. It's obviously not real. It doesn't literally transport us, but it's like a computer program. We wear these—" Putting her phone down, she grabbed a small wooden box from her drawer and placed them on my lap. "Eye lenses and earbud sensors. A bit like when Vaughn plays PlayStation, you know? He wears the headset and headphones? He sees the game all around him. He's immersed."

Opening the box, I glanced at the typical small containers for eye lenses and the earbuds. "And you want to play a computer game?"

She blushed. "I want to play a game...with you."

I tensed as a wash of her emotions caught me by surprise. My condition allowed me to eavesdrop on my wife. I knew when she was pissed at me for leaving my polo gear untended and dirty on our chaise lounge. I knew when she stared at me with love when I kissed and played with our children. And I knew when she wanted me. The hot warmth that spilled from her was full of need and invitation.

In a way, she couldn't hide from me. She couldn't lie if I'd annoyed her or pretend things were okay when they weren't.

But now...

I couldn't understand what she felt.

She was excited, nervous, intrigued, turned on.

Afraid.

I looked harder at the sensors she'd given me, trying to figure out what this meant. What had Sully created here?

"You want me, Needle. I can sense that. But I don't understand the fear."

She looked down at the white bedspread before forcing herself to meet my eyes and blurt everything. "You must've heard the rumours too. About Sully's fantasy world that he's using on his Rapture islands? That he can code any kink and insert a couple to do whatever they want? All we have to do is wear those lenses and earbuds, choose a fantasy and press this button." She showed me on the phone, small icons of BDSM dungeons, office desks, kinky playrooms, and outdoor picnics revealed the nature of each erotic fantasy.

My cock twitched in interest. But before I could agree or disagree, Nila said, "There's something else."

My eyebrows shot up. "What exactly?"

She pulled a small stopper bottle from her back pocket. "This."

I took it from her, inspecting the smoky glass, before unscrewing the lid to smell the contents.

It smelled vaguely sweet and flowery—like the exotic orchids growing in our greenhouses. "What is it?"

"*Cinta*. I think Eleanor told me it's Indonesian for love."

"So it *is* a drug."

She nodded reluctantly, knowing my tangled relationship with drugs, doctors, and being called crazy.

In the past, I was crazy, and no one had a cure.

Now, I was sane and could balance my nature so I could function in the real world. I wouldn't jeopardise that for fucking anything.

Screwing the bottle shut, I shoved it at her. "I'm happy to fuck you in whatever position you want. We'll get the hounds and Wings and go for a run in the woods if that's what you're after. I will never say no to you, nor would I ever want to. But...I'm not taking any substance. *Especially* something that Sullivan has cooked. He's too proficient at creating things that actually work, unlike the other big pharma with their useless promises."

"This is different." She rolled the bottle in her fingers. "It won't change you. It doesn't do a thing apart from work on what's already between us." Crawling on her hands and knees, she didn't stop until she splayed her legs on either side of my hips and straddled me.

The instant her body heat came close, my instincts kicked in, and our lust that always infected us sprang into full attention. Grabbing her hips, I pushed her down, rocking her along my rapidly hardening cock.

Her eyes hooded, placing her hands on my shoulders and bending to kiss her way along my throat. "It's an aphrodisiac."

I chuckled darkly, thrusting my erection against the seam of her jeans. "Does it feel like I need an aphrodisiac? You are the only thing I need to get hard."

"I know." She writhed on me, making my head swim. "But I also know that you can't fully be in your own thoughts. You feel me. You feel whoever is close by. Your thoughts are always stretched in so many directions through no fault of your own. And I want…" She licked her way up my neck, making me groan. "I want to give you a night where the only thing you think about is how much you want to fuck me."

I jerked as her teeth sank around my ear. "Believe me, Nila, that's all I'm thinking about right now."

"No, it's not." She pulled back, her skin flushed and so fucking beautiful. "You're thinking about Kes and Emma because I can still hear them bickering down the corridor. You're keeping me safe by scanning the hall for trespassers and keeping your perception open. I know how hard the masquerade was for you. I know you've struggled to shed the thoughts of guests. I want you to just be *you*. To only have one voice inside your head." Her lips landed on mine, kissing me hard.

I gave in to her, allowing her to dictate how deep, how fast. While she kissed me, I unbuttoned her shirt and shoved it down her arms. Her bra unclipped at the back, freeing her breasts and making my teeth ache to bite her nipples.

But then she was gone, leaving me hard and impatient. "Come back here."

"Put these on first." Holding out the lenses and earbuds, she cocked her head. "Come on, Kite. One night. Trust me."

I paused, glaring at her hand and the outstretched sensors. I trusted her over everyone, but I also had no intention of ingesting a drug Sullivan had made.

I'd learned that the hard way.

Focusing on Nila, working past her wash of lust, I pickpocketed through her other emotions. I tried not to trespass on her thoughts too much. After all, being married to a man like me gave her no privacy whatsoever. However, she accepted who I was when she vowed her life to mine, and in this case, I had a right to rifle.

Once again, there was trepidation and excitement, but the fear had gone, drowned out by wet desire. She was telling the truth that she wanted me. A lot. And she wanted to be alone with me in a way we'd never been able to be before.

Coming closer, she touched my cheek softly. "It's just something fun, Jet. Nothing more. I would *never* ask you to do something that could jeopardize everything we've worked so hard to build." Her tone throbbed with honesty. Honesty that matched her fierce, affectionate ownership over me and my condition.

"I love you." She bent to kiss me again.

And I couldn't fight the swell of everlasting love.

I kissed her back, nodding slowly. "Okay, Needle. If it's what you want."

Pulling away, she stayed silent as she tipped my head back and carefully placed the eye lenses over my right and left eye. I blinked against the obstruction, regretting my approval as she attempted to put the buds in my ears.

"Here, let me." I pushed her away gently, ensuring the buds were in correctly.

With slightly shaking hands, she placed eye lenses over her own pupils before brushing aside her hair and inserting the earbuds. When she was done, she looked at me as she had the first night I'd met her.

The night of her Milan fashion show. She'd been so nervous and eager to please. So innocent and fragile. And I'd snatched, stolen, and broken her.

Fuck.

Wrapping my hands in her hair, I jerked her into me, kissing her deeply. Pouring my well-worn apologies down her throat.

She kissed me back, her hands busy between us.

I was swept up in her tongue, carried away by the rapidly increasing passion between us that I didn't sense what she was about to do until it was too late.

She pulled away for a fraction of a second and tipped her head back, squeezing a droplet of whatever liquid was in the stopper vial. She swallowed and added another, pressing her mouth to mine instantly, kissing me with the sugary, flowery drug.

She passed it to me.

It burned my tongue.

I pushed her away, cursing her. "What the hell did you just do? I agreed to the game, not the drug."

"Trust me." She shrugged out of her shirt and wriggled off me to remove her jeans and underwear. "I'm trying to give you a night of freedom."

My heart pounded harder as she straddled me again, naked and ready in my arms.

My lust ignited with a thousand fires. She was so fucking beautiful, so perfect, so *mine.*

She'd pushed me into something I didn't want but her

intentions were pure and protective.

"You'll pay for that." Tugging her hair back, I kept her prone while I kissed her. "I'm already free when I'm with you. I don't need anything else." My other hand explored places of her that I knew by heart yet felt like the first time as I slid a finger inside her and felt her delicious heat.

She moaned and welcomed me to take more. "God, punish me all you want."

"I have every intention of it."

My control seemed to fade with every heartbeat.

Every second that ticked past, I fell a little more into her.

My cock grew harder.

My awareness narrowed until it revolved entirely around her.

The outside world was gone.

There were no more webs that I cast to listen to members of this household. No worry over my children. No history of what'd happened in this hall.

Just Nila.

And fuck, I wanted her.

So.

Fucking.

Much.

She gasped as I flipped her onto her back and laid between her spread legs. I scrambled to shove my pyjama bottoms down, desperation making me clumsy.

Nila moaned as I finally freed myself. My cock throbbing to fill her.

Unlike our previous connections, this time I wasn't swayed by her desire for me. I couldn't tap into what she was feeling because my own emotions were amplified.

Drenched and dark, my lust grew thick and loud in my skull.

What a novelty to only feel myself and not someone else.

What a fucking gift to be free from the constant *noise*.

I groaned and kissed her, pouring lust down her throat.

Her one hand scratched my back, locking on my ass and pulling me up and into her. We both grunted as we connected, thrust, joined.

I'd never ever get sick of being inside my wife.

Her back bowed as I shoved upward, filling her, taking her. My heart hammered, and I couldn't get enough. I wanted to come now, but I also wanted to delay. I wanted this feeling of absolute obsession to last as long as it could.

Then again, I felt like I could come again and again. That I could come all night because that was how much I fucking lusted after this woman.

I was only vaguely aware of her other hand shooting across the bed and fisting her phone. Barely coherent under the wash of hot need as she breathed into my ear, "You're free to just be you tonight, Kite. No distractions. Just us."

She kissed me hard.

She pressed the button on her phone.

The world went white.

Hawksridge Hall disappeared.

Static hissing wiped away any memory of being an Empath.

And when colour and solidity returned, I blinked in an entirely new dimension.

Nila was beneath me.

My cock was firmly inside her.

She was just as beautiful as always.

Yet we were on a rooftop on a pile of Persian blankets, the sand-coloured dwellings and elaborate stained glass lights of Marrakesh strewn beneath us.

And for the first time in my godforsaken life, I didn't feel another person. I didn't sense their thoughts or pick up on opinions I didn't want.

It was quiet inside.

Blissfully, incredibly *quiet.*

Absolute gratefulness filled me. Nila's own desire for me trickled through the quietness. Her thoughts as familiar as my own, our lust mirroring pieces of each other. Our bodies were linked, but our minds were threaded on a level we'd never found before.

We were alone.

Just us.

And I was free to take her in every way possible.

Sucking in a breath, I pressed a kiss on Nila's lips. "I could get used to this." I kissed her harder, giving in to the serenity and pleasure she'd given me.

"Oh, God. Me too." She arched her back, making me fill her deeper. "Let's do this every night."

I chuckled.

I rocked up.

I fell all over again.

We both smiled, knowing this would be an evening we'd

never forget.

A night where the world fell apart, freedom was found in a virtual reality dimension, and a drug cooked by a friend gave me the greatest gift imaginable.

He gave me silence.

He gave me peace.

He gave me the chance to love my wife exactly as she deserved.

Thoroughly and wholeheartedly.

Forever.

* * * *

Thank you so much for reading Sully's Fantasy.
If you haven't met Nila and Jethro, their romance is complete and ready to read in the **New York Times Bestselling Series, Indebted Series.**
It wasn't all happiness for those two. There were a lot of debts, pain, and betrayal. First book is FREE on all platforms.

Don't forget there is one more Novella in Goddess Isles!
Jinx's Fantasy *releases 25*[th] *August and will feature cameos by Elder and Pim (Dollar Series). See the cover and blurb below.*

Thanks again and have a wonderful week.
Pepper.
X

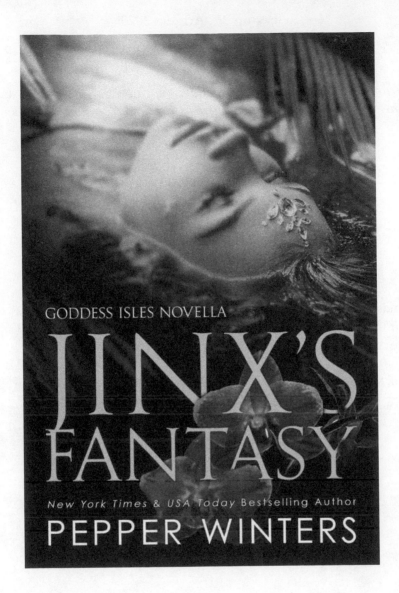

GODDESS ISLES NOVELLA

JINX'S FANTASY

New York Times & USA Today Bestselling Author

PEPPER WINTERS

Releasing 25ˢᵗ August 2020

From New York Times Bestseller, Pepper Winters, comes a spin-off novella featuring Sully and Jinx from the USA Today Bestselling Series, Goddess Isles

"A marriage born from slavery and secrets.
A happily ever after like no other."

Sullivan Sinclair has a wife who shares his wildness and desires. To others, she is regal and perfect on his arm. To him, she is a goddess with dirty appetites that need to be fulfilled.

Eleanor Sinclair has a husband who allows her darkest fantasies to come true. Aboard their new luxury yacht, purchased for their cluster of islands called Rapture, he suggests a game of seduction. Another play in Euphoria.

Sea, sky, or sand—thanks to Sully's unique playground, they can play anywhere. They can change their appearances, distort time, and indulge in romance with no rules.
Eleanor granted Sully's his ultimate fantasy.
Now, it's Sully's turn to grant hers.

Release Date: 25ˢᵗ August 2020

OTHER BOOKS AVAILABLE FROM PEPPER WINTERS

FREE BOOKS
Debt Inheritance (Indebted Series #1)
Tears of Tess (Monsters in the Dark #1)
Pennies (Dollar Series #1)

BOOKS IN KINDLE UNLIMITED
Destroyed (Standalone)

Dollar Series
Pennies
Dollars
Hundreds
Thousands
Millions

Truth & Lies Duet
Crown of Lies
Throne of Truth

Pure Corruption Duet
Ruin & Rule
Sin & Suffer

Indebted Series
Debt Inheritance
First Debt
Second Debt
Third Debt
Fourth Debt
Final Debt
Indebted Epilogue

Monsters in the Dark Trilogy
Tears of Tess
Quintessentially Q

CPSIA information can be obtained
at www.ICGtesting.com
Printed in the USA
LVHW091945110721
692415LV00008B/1344